"Maybe there's something out there . . .

After they ran several hundred yards, they stopped to catch their breaths. Their chests ached. Kirkland's face was still bleeding from the dog bites.

"We're on the flatland," Miles said. "The ground is hard."

Kirkland gazed behind them. "It will be bloody if those hounds get us."

Miles peered at the glowing red eyes. "Maybe we scared them. They're finally afraid of us."

Kirkland turned to gaze out over the flat, dark, unknown plain. "Maybe there's something out there that scares them even more," he said.

Attack!

Clay Coleman

HarperPaperbacks
A Division of HarperCollins*Publishers*

For Tom

This is a work of fiction. The characters, incidents, and dialogues are products of the author's imagination and are not to be construed as real. Any resemblance to actual events or persons, living or dead, is entirely coincidental.

HarperPaperbacks *A Division of* HarperCollins*Publishers*
10 East 53rd Street, New York, N.Y. 10022

Produced by Daniel Weiss Associates, Inc.
33 West 17th Street, New York, New York 10011.

RL 4.8   IL 008–012
First printing: December, 1990

Printed in the United States of America

HarperPaperbacks and colophon are trademarks of HarperCollins*Publishers*

10 9 8 7 6 5 4 3 2 1

Attack!

.

One

Len Hayden gazed out at the breaking blue waves of the Pacific Ocean. The fifteen-year-old boy from Portsmouth, New Hampshire, was searching for signs of trouble in the red glow of dawn. He was expecting an attack from the hostile island to the south. Len and his companions had escaped from it once, but he knew they were still not safe from the horror they had so narrowly escaped.

Len had been on the beach all night, having drawn the short straw when they divided up the shifts. The lulling, ominous roar of the surf made the darkness more frightening than he had ever imagined it could be.

As the tropical sunrise grew brighter, Len felt better. Somehow, the light made it easier for him to stand sentinel over his own island prison. No matter what happened, Len would never be able to call the island home.

Len shifted his feet in the sand. He turned back toward the compound, which was hidden from his view on the volcanic plateau behind him. The jungle around him had come to life a little. Bright birds flitted in the cool breezes that stirred the trees and vines.

The others would be awake soon. Miles would take the shift after Len. Kirkland and Augie would make breakfast over a fire.

A chill spread through Len's body. He could not accept being marooned on the South Seas island. The compound, which had been built by research scientists, still gave him the creeps. With the approval of the United States government, the group of scientists had run experiments on the worst hardened criminals they could find. Their Proteus Project had attempted to develop a serum that would turn bad men into good citizens. But the Proteus Project had failed miserably. The criminals had only gotten worse. They had rebelled against the scientists and driven them away. Now the mutants lived in a secret camp on Lost Island.

Len looked out over the water again. He scanned the choppy waters for signs of Meat Hook and his men. Meat Hook was the mutant leader. He was the one who had attacked before, when Len and the others had been lucky enough to drive him away.

Len still had bad dreams about that first assault. He could still see Miles on the motorized hang glider, dropping gasoline bombs on the unholy forces. Meat Hook had not counted on the castaway boys being so tough. The scientists had left behind large caches of supplies in the compound. Len and the others had made the best of their circumstances. But they were all afraid of what lay to the south on Lost Island.

Len looked to the sky, hoping to see a search plane. Why hadn't someone come to find them? Had the authorities given up? Their plane had been due in Honolulu weeks ago. Hadn't anyone cared enough to send out a rescue team? He hadn't seen a plane in the sky. Maybe, for some reason relating to the Proteus Project, the authorities wanted to avoid these islands. *That means they'll never find us*, Len thought.

The waves broke over the sand. Water rushed up toward Len's feet. He stepped back. As the water receded, a few large crabs scurried through the shallow, glassy flow.

Len waded into the water, trying to capture the crabs. Miles had told him to grab them by the claws so they couldn't bite. Len's fingers closed around the back of a claw, but the crab was too fast. It turned and clamped down on the palm of his hand.

"Ow!"

He jumped back. Blood poured from the cut on his palm. He stomped the water, trying to even the score with the hostile crustacean.

"That's no way to catch your breakfast, Hayden!"

A shadow fell beside Len. He turned back to see Miles Bookman standing on the beach. Miles had come to take the next watch.

Len gestured to the surf with his bloody hand. "Let's see you do better, Bookman!"

Miles laughed and started into the water. He dipped his hands into the frothing surf. Within a few minutes he had flipped three large crabs onto the beach, where they squirmed helplessly on their backs.

"How's that?" Miles called from the water.

Len grimaced. "At least you aren't a casualty like me."

Miles waded out of the water. He broke off the claws and put the crabs into a small sack. He was a year younger than Len, but sometimes Miles showed skills and intelligence beyond his age.

"Take them back to camp when you go up," Miles said.

Len nodded. "I'm going to keep trying until I learn how to catch those things without losing a finger."

Miles didn't gloat at his friend's failure. Instead, he turned his wary eyes toward the south. He was looking for the same sails that Len feared. Sails on the horizon would mean trouble.

"No sign of the mutants?"

Len shook his head. "All clear. For now. You think—"

"They'll come again," Miles replied.

"Yeah, I know. But when? We haven't seen any sign of them since you chased them with those gas bombs."

Miles smiled a little, taking pride in his accomplishment. "We sent them packing that time."

"We caught them off guard," Len said. "They weren't expecting us to fight back. They won't be so careless when they come after us again."

"No, they won't. That means we have to be ready."

"We've got to get off this island," Len replied.

Miles looked at his friend. "We will. We'll be back at Dover Academy in time for the fall semester. We'll be in old man Henderson's science class, telling him all about it. I know that old buzzard won't believe a word we say."

"I wouldn't believe it, either," Len replied.

They were quiet for a moment.

Len began to wonder about his family back in New Hampshire. His father would already be at the bookshop, unpacking the books that had arrived the day before. His mother would be getting ready for work at the hospital, where she was a nurse on the day shift. Sarah, his younger sister, was probably dressing for school. Len wished he could see them before the mutants attacked again from the south.

"What's on your mind?" Miles asked.

Len sighed. "Just thinking about home."

Miles frowned. He wasn't as lucky with his

family. Miles lived in the dormitory at the academy. His parents were divorced.

Miles's father was Sir Charles Bookman, the famous British photojournalist. His mother was Katherine Wainwright, a TV actress, and she lived in Los Angeles. Miles rarely got to see either of his parents. He did not seem to miss them as much as Len missed his family.

Miles gazed up at the clear sky. "Another perfect day."

"It can't be that perfect," Len replied. "There are no rescue planes. We're trapped by that mountain. The high rocks won't even let us follow the shoreline. This little stretch of beach is all we have."

Miles shrugged. "I know," he said softly.

Sometimes Len thought that Miles enjoyed being marooned on the hellish island. He liked camping out. It was an adventure to him.

"Maybe they gave up on us," Len said, voicing his worst fear.

"Maybe. But there's a lot of water out here, Hayden. They'll have to search for a long time. And we've got our marker out."

Len looked at the large SOS that they had constructed from palm fronds and coconuts. "I hope they can see it from the air."

"They'll see it," Miles replied. "Those letters are ten feet high."

Len shuddered. "I just hope they get here before Meat Hook and the other mutoids decide to attack us again. Those guys are seriously crazed. How about that guy with the helmet!"

They both shivered at the thought of Bullet Head, a three-hundred-pound killer who wore a rounded steel helmet over his bald head. The deadly behemoth must have risen from some hideous nightmare.

Len and Miles had been captives on Lost Island. Kirkland and Joey Wolfe had come with the flare gun to set the huts on fire and free them. They had managed to escape in the confusion that followed. And they did not want to be captured again.

"I keep thinking about Joey and Vinnie," Miles offered. "I wish they weren't dead."

"Even Vinnie?" Len asked.

Miles sighed. "He was rude, but he didn't deserve to die."

Len wanted to change the subject. He didn't like to think about Joey and Vinnie. There had also been other boys who had perished in the plane crash and in the first encounter with the mutants. He could still see little Pee Wee being hoisted on a stake by the one called Cannibal.

"Are Kirkland and Augie up yet?" Len asked.

Miles shook his head. "No, they're still sleeping. I woke up early."

Suddenly Len stiffened and pointed toward the water. "Bookman, check it out."

Miles squinted toward the horizon. "What—"

"See them?" Len replied. "On the water. A bunch of them."

He pointed toward the shapes that were cutting across the surface of the sea.

Miles felt his stomach turn. "This is it."

What looked like small sails were knifing toward them from the southern horizon.

"The mutants!" Miles cried.

Len's legs went weak as the dark shapes drew closer to the island.

Lieutenant Branch Colgan, United States Coast Guard pilot, waited in the receiving room of his base commander's office. With every strand of his wavy black hair in place and his skin bronzed from the sun, Colgan looked ruggedly handsome in his military dress uniform. He wanted to look his best for this confrontation with his superior officer.

Colgan had arrived at the commander's office shortly after the call for reveille. He had skipped breakfast in the officers' mess. The task at hand was too important to let anything get in the way. Colgan hoped that the base commander would now put to an end his weeks of frustration.

The outer door opened. Colgan stood up. The commander's aide came in with a briefcase under his arm. The aide, an ensign, saluted the lieutenant, who returned the salute.

The aide squinted at Colgan. "You're awfully

early, sir. Do you have an appointment to see Commander Nickles?"

"No, not an official appointment," Colgan replied. "But I need to see the commander as soon as possible. It's very important."

The aide moved around behind the reception desk. "Commander Nickles has a heavy schedule this morning. May I ask the nature of your business?"

"It's a private matter," Colgan replied.

"I see. Well, I don't know if the commander will be in this morning. I believe he—"

The door opened again, and Commander Robert Nickles strode into the office. Colgan saluted the gray-haired man, who was still in excellent physical condition. The aide also saluted.

Nickles waved at them. "Good morning, gentlemen."

The aide caught his boss's eye. "Sir, Lieutenant Colgan wants to make an appointment to see you."

Colgan snapped to attention. "Good morning, sir."

Commander Nickles turned to him. "At ease, Lieutenant."

Colgan relaxed into parade rest. "I'm sorry to bother you so early, sir. But I'm here on a matter of great importance."

Nickles peered at the lieutenant. "Colgan? Aren't you the pilot who found Senator Williams when his boat was stalled off Lanai?"

"Yes, sir. That was me."

"Good work, Lieutenant," the commander replied. "That senator couldn't stop talking about you. My guess is that you're in for a promotion. How long have you been in the Coast Guard?"

Colgan shrugged. "Five years, sir."

"Are you a lifer?"

"I hope to be," Colgan replied.

The lieutenant tried not to smile at the thought of a promotion. He had only been doing his job when he rescued the stranded politician. Colgan wanted to keep doing his duty in the service of the Coast Guard. That was the reason he had come to appeal to his commanding officer.

The aide tried to steer around the lieutenant. "Sir, I can make another appointment if—"

Nickles clapped Colgan on the shoulder. "Nonsense. I always have time for the good men in my command. Step into my office, Lieutenant."

The commander's office spoke of a life of military service. He sat behind a huge oak desk that was covered with mementos of his career. Colgan took his place in a chair on the other side of the desk.

"Would you like some coffee?" Nickles asked.

"No, sir. If you don't object, Commander, I'll get right to the point."

Nickles gave a nod. "Good! I appreciate directness from my officers. Speak freely, Lieutenant."

Colgan filled his lungs with air. "A few weeks back, almost a month ago, an old C-47 disappeared on a flight from Majoru, in the Marshalls, to Oahu. The plane was a charter. It carried a load of passengers, some of whom were the children of military personnel. They were involved in some kind of rehabilitation program for youth offenders—kids who had gotten into trouble on military bases."

Nickles frowned. "I'm familiar with Operation Involvement, Lieutenant. But I don't see what—"

"Please, sir. Let me finish."

The commander nodded, even though the frown remained on his face.

"So far there hasn't been any trace of the C-47 or the passengers," Colgan went on. "I believe the plane went down in Omega quadrant."

The commander bristled and shifted nervously in his seat.

"I've tried to get permission to fly into Omega quadrant," Colgan said. "But the area is restricted to all military flights."

"As it should be," Nickles replied.

Colgan leaned forward. "With all due respect, sir, those kids could be lost in Omega quadrant. I've applied for clearance to go in there, but I've been turned down several times. I can't get permission to search the area. I was hoping you'd—"

Nickles looked away. "I can't help you, Lieutenant."

"Sir, I can appreciate the—"

Nickles turned to glare at him. "You've said enough, Lieutenant. As of this moment, I won't hear another word. You're dismissed."

"But—"

"That's an order, Lieutenant Colgan!"

Colgan leaned forward in his chair. "We have to search Omega quadrant, Commander. If those kids are in there—and I have a hunch they are—we can't just leave them. They'll die. They may be dead already."

Nickles slammed his fist on the desk. "I will not have my command influenced by hunches, Lieutenant!"

"I know they're in there, sir. I can feel it in my bones."

Nickles waved him off. "Dismissed, Lieutenant. I won't say it again. This is out of my hands. I couldn't send you into Omega quadrant even if I wanted to. And you probably won't get permission from anyone else. My advice to you is to leave it alone. Is that clear?"

Colgan stood up and saluted. He did not wait for Commander Nickles to salute him back. He turned and stormed out of the office, past the gawking aide.

When the lieutenant was outside, he wiped the nervous sweat from his brow. It was going to be another warm day in the Hawaiian Islands. But Lieutenant Branch Colgan was not concerned about the weather. He had to find a way to get into Omega quadrant.

"The senator," he said under his breath.

Maybe the politician could help him.

Colgan did not care if he had to go over his commander's head.

The lieutenant wouldn't rest until he found a way to complete his urgent mission.

Len and Miles stood on the beach, gawking at the dark shapes that cut through the water.

Len was frozen. "We better get Kirkland."

Miles nodded, but neither one of them could move. They were transfixed by the movement beyond the waves, the gray triangles glinting in the morning sun.

"Wait a minute," Len said. "Those are fish."

Miles saw gray rounded backs break the surface of the water. "Dolphins!" he exclaimed. "Pacific bottlenose dolphins. They aren't fish—they're mammals, like whales."

They watched the graceful creatures move effortlessly in the blue water. There were at least a dozen of them. The group came close enough for the boys to hear the sounds of their breathing.

"Incredible," said Len. "I thought those fins were sails on the horizon. They looked so real."

They watched the dolphins for a few minutes. The sleek, aquatic swimmers cut through a school of baitfish. The baitfish shot out of the water as the dolphins began to feed voraciously.

"That's what'll happen to us if we don't get off this island," said Len with a sigh. "Meat Hook and his boys will eat us alive."

From behind them came a familiar voice. "Man, I've had some bad luck before, but this is too much. Stuck on this rock with you preps. Those death-punks running wild all over the place. I guess I'm just a bad-luck kinda guy."

They turned to see Kirkland, his hands on his hips, staring at them. Kirkland was a rugged kid, older than Len and Miles. He had gotten into trouble at an army base school by slugging a history teacher. Nobody had cared that the teacher had hit Kirkland first. Kirkland had been sent to the delinquent work camp in the Marshall Islands for his punishment.

Len kept silent. He was a little bit afraid of Kirkland. The older boy was unpredictable. Kirkland could be violent, and he had the muscle to act on his temper.

"I keep thinking about Vinnie and Joey," Kirkland said. "I've been having nightmares about them."

Miles was not sure what to say to Kirkland. He had also been having bad dreams that replayed the first encounter with Meat Hook and the other bandits. Sometimes he woke up in the middle of the night after dreaming about some horrible torture.

Len looked back toward the jungle. "Where's Augie?"

"I sent him to pick oranges," Kirkland replied. "He's okay."

"Maybe we ought to help him," Miles offered. "I mean, he's only twelve years old—"

Kirkland shot Miles a dirty look. "Who put you in charge, prep?"

Miles stared at Kirkland, but said nothing.

Len wanted to remind Kirkland that Miles had been the one who found the motorized hang glider. Meat Hook hadn't expected the gas bombs from the air. Miles deserved some credit for saving them from the bandits.

Len also felt that he and Miles should have a say in all matters that concerned their survival. But Kirkland was not about to let democracy reign over their predicament. He was bigger and stronger. As long as Kirkland could beat them up, he called the shots.

Of course, they could gang up on him, but that would not help their chances of survival.

Len peered toward the jungle. "Lucky thing about those orange trees. I wonder what other kinds of plants those scientists left behind."

"Plants *and* animals," Miles replied. "I'll look at those records in the lab again. Those scientists left behind the log of their experiments."

Kirkland did not seem to be listening. He turned toward the wreckage of the hang glider. The glider lay hidden in shrubbery at the head of the beach. They had dragged it there the day after their fight with the bandits. The boys had not yet tried to repair the silk and aluminum craft.

Kirkland started across the sand. "Come on, dweebs. It's time to take a look at the glider."

Len and Miles hesitated. Kirkland turned back and told them to get it in gear. They followed him toward the wreck of the glider.

"I hope he doesn't turn into Carl Caveman again," Len said in a low voice. "He was all right there for a while."

"Humor him," Miles replied. "This island's big enough for all of us."

"Thanks for reminding me, Bookman."

They encircled the twisted mass of the downed glider. There were holes in the silk surface of the wings, where Meat Hook had fired on it with a rifle. Miles trembled at the memory of the battle. His days as a pilot had almost ended in a hail of bullets.

Kirkland bent over to look at the engine of the glider. "Shot straight through," he said with a sigh. "Probably took out the cylinder. Meat Hook must have been using steel-jacketed shells."

Len wiped the sweat from his brow. "Awesome. I wonder if he's got any more weapons like that."

"This thing looks shot to me," Kirkland said.

"You know about engines and stuff?" Miles asked.

16

"Yeah," Kirkland replied defensively. "I took auto shop in school. What's it to you?"

"Just asking," Miles replied.

Kirkland studied the one-cylinder engine on the glider. "This thing isn't even as complicated as a car motor. It's more like something off a lawn mower."

"Can we fix it?" Len asked.

Kirkland exhaled. "I don't know, kid." They started to raise the glider from the sand. It wasn't heavy, but the engine weighed enough to make the task awkward. Something made a cracking noise as they hoisted the craft.

"Stop!" Kirkland cried.

Miles grimaced. "Maybe—" He stopped short, not wanting to challenge Kirkland's authority.

"Spit it out," Kirkland said.

Miles tried not to sound too much like a know-it-all. "Well, we could take it apart. Carry it up in pieces."

Kirkland was about to voice his approval for Miles's idea, but he never got out the words.

A horrible, piercing scream resounded from the jungle.

Kirkland wheeled, gaping wide-eyed in the direction of the cry. "Augie!"

The younger boy was hollering from the jungle. His cries sounded desperate, as if something were about to swallow him whole.

Two

Joey Wolfe opened his eyes to another dreadful day in the bamboo cage. His cell hung over the hideous compound of Meat Hook and the other bandit warriors on Lost Island. Joey had been locked in captivity ever since he and Vinnie Pelligrino were caught during the first confrontation with the bandits.

Joey turned toward the palm and bamboo huts that were scattered about the compound, which was hidden in a lagoon behind a wall of volcanic rock. One small channel led out of the lagoon. Thick jungle spread behind the beach. A search plane would have a lot of trouble spotting the unholy gathering.

"Good morning, Chief Worried Cat. Did you have a good sleep?"

The voice rose from below the cage. The one called Cannibal leered at him in the morning shadows, as he stirred a huge caldron that steamed over a fire.

"You look sad, Chief Worried Cat. Don't worry. Your friend isn't in here." He paused, while he stirred. "He's not sweet enough. And besides, we're vegetarians."

Joey spat at him. "Chew on a clamshell."

Cannibal flashed a brown gap-toothed smile. " 'One little, one little, one little Indian. One little Indian boy.' What tribe are you, Worried Cat?"

Joey made a hostile gesture.

Cannibal laughed as if he had just heard the funniest joke in the world.

Joey turned away from the hateful laughter. He was half Cherokee, but he would never tell that to the weird animal who stirred the caldron.

Joey's mother still lived on a reservation in North Carolina. He had gotten into trouble because he kept running away from his father and the army base where they lived. He had only wanted to go back to the reservation to live with his mother. He hated living on the army base. When they caught him the last time, they had sent him to the work camp in the Marshall Islands as punishment for his frequent departures.

The plane crash had left him lost in the Pacific with the others. And there didn't seem to be any hope of escape, unless he could get word to Len and Miles and Kirkland, on the other island. They surely thought he and Vinnie were dead by now. But how could he send them a message?

Joey scanned the lagoon, counting the small boats and huts. Meat Hook and his men were rebuilding their forces. Kirkland had turned the place into a raging inferno with the flare gun they had salvaged from the plane. The others had been able to escape, but Joey and Vinnie had not been so lucky.

The camp was still quiet. Meat Hook and the others were recovering from a battle outside the lagoon. Kirkland and Len and Miles had defeated them somehow. What had happened out there?

Joey leaned back against the bamboo bars. He looked over at Vinnie Pelligrino. The red-haired boy was still sleeping. Joey moved over to check the wound in Vinnie's stomach.

Vinnie had taken an aluminum arrow during the fight with Meat Hook's marauders. Joey had stayed behind to help him. At first, Joey had worried that Vinnie was going to die, but the tough kid had surprised him by hanging on day after day. Vinnie was weak, but he was alive.

"Don't die on me, Vinnie," Joey whispered. "I won't let you do it."

Vinnie stirred, opening his green eyes. "Joey—" He coughed and asked for water. Joey lifted a coconut shell to his dry lips. Vinnie raised his head, sipping the lukewarm liquid.

"You hungry?" Joey asked.

Vinnie nodded weakly. Joey fed him a piece of banana. The bandits had provided them with food and water since their capture. Joey figured that Meat Hook was fattening them up for the kill—or something worse. He didn't want to imagine what Cannibal might do to them.

One of the other boys, Pee Wee, had been killed, and his body had disappeared without a trace. Cannibal had dragged him into the woods.

Vinnie grabbed his arm. "Somebody—help us—rescue—help—" he muttered.

"Sure, Vinnie. Kirkland is still alive—at least I think so. He did something to these mutants."

Vinnie closed his eyes. Joey treated his wound again, then moved away. It was a miracle that the arrow had not killed Vinnie. Maybe there would be more miracles around the corner.

A gong resounded in the camp. The fat, ugly bandit known as Bullet Head, steel helmet in hand, stood at attention beside the gong in front of the largest grass hut, near the edge of the lagoon.

After Bullet Head rang the gong three times, Meat Hook emerged from the hut. The gong was the call to reveille, like an army bugle, Meat Hook's way of stirring his platoon to life. They came out of their new huts. Most of the structures had been rebuilt after Kirkland had torched the old ones with the flare gun from the downed C-47.

Meat Hook stood proud and tall in front of his hut. A tattoo of a bald eagle covered his rippling chest. A long scar ran down one side of his face. Burn wounds still covered a great deal of his body. He had come back with the burns after the battle outside the lagoon, in which Kirkland and the others had defeated the mutants.

The other bandits gathered in front of Meat Hook's hut. Joey counted twenty of them. They were also covered with hideous wounds. Many of them had treated their wounds with coconut oil.

How had Kirkland repelled such a strong invading force?

Meat Hook raised his hand. He held an iron hook in his fist. The end of the hook had been sharpened to a shiny point.

"Brothers!" Meat Hook cried. "We are strong again!"

The chant rose up over the camp, chilling Joey. "Strong again! Strong again!"

Bullet Head slammed his rounded steel helmet against the gong. The chant died. The bandits hung on Meat Hook's every word.

The iron hook waved in the air. "Brothers! We must have revenge. Our enemies must die!"

"Die! Die!"

Meat Hook pointed his weapon at the cage.

"See our enemies, brothers! They have come as children. The children must die!"

"The children must die!"

"Kill them!"

Sweat broke over Joey's forehead. The mutants turned to look at him. They wanted blood. Joey could see it in their eyes.

"Brothers!" Meat Hook cried. "We are strong, but we must grow stronger. We are not ready to strike yet."

"Stronger!"

"Kill them now!"

"When will we strike?" one of them called out.

"Soon," the bandit leader replied. "Soon! We cannot be vanquished!" Meat Hook cried. "The children cannot stop us this time."

The bandits cheered.

Joey wondered if he had died and gone to a dark place underground. Hell could not be any worse than the bandit camp.

Meat Hook waved the iron hook over the group. "Go, brothers! Find your strength. Prepare for the day when we can bring death to our hated enemies."

"Death to our enemies!" Bullet Head cried, raising both hands.

"Death to our enemies!" the bandits cried in unison.

Bullet Head slammed his helmet against the gong. The bandit warriors began to disperse. They filed by Cannibal's fire. The white-faced ghoul served their breakfast as they went past him.

Joey knew what was coming next. Some of the warriors would practice with their cross-bows and kung fu throwing stars. Others would work on the sailing vessels that made up the evil armada. The routine had been the same every day since the battle.

Bullet Head and Meat Hook strode toward Joey's cage. He could see the hideous red wounds all over them. Meat Hook wore a black patch over his right eye.

Vinnie stirred to life for a few moments. "What? Joey—"

"Nothing," Joey replied. "Captain Hook is stirring up the troops again. Go back to sleep."

Vinnie closed his eyes.

Meat Hook stopped below the cage and pointed his weapon at Joey. "You! You shall suffer the sins of your brothers! You shall pay. Retribution is at hand."

"In your ear, Freddy Krueger!" Joey cried.

Joey tried to be brave, even though his whole body was trembling.

Bullet Head uttered a hateful laugh. "I kill him now!"

Meat Hook shook his head. "No! He must suffer first."

Cannibal moved next to his exalted leader. "Sire, shall I lower the cage?"

"Yes," Meat Hook replied. "Lower the cage!"

Cannibal untied the thick rope.

Joey grabbed the bamboo bars, hanging on tightly as the cage inched down to the ground below.

Len and Miles followed Kirkland to the edge of the rain forest and the sound of Augie's screaming. The forest grew thicker above them, encroaching over the narrow path.

Kirkland stopped at the line of palm trees. "Augie! Can you hear me? Augie, where are you?"

The younger boy's cries for help echoed through the rain forest.

"He's in the clearing!" Miles cried.

"I hope so," Kirkland said under his breath. Kirkland started onto the path that led deeper into the forest.

Len hesitated and grabbed his friend's arm. "I hope those mutants haven't come back."

Miles didn't reply. He followed Kirkland on the path. Len came after them. His legs were still weak, but he managed to make headway through the tangles that hung over the trail.

"Help me!" Augie cried. "Somebody help me!"

They were getting closer to the younger boy. Len could hear him crying. They burst into the clearing where the orange trees grew.

Augie cowered beside a tree trunk, trembling and sobbing. "Kirkland! Help me!"

Kirkland looked around the clearing, but he

could see no sign of a threat. "Augie, what's your problem?"

Miles knelt beside Augie, who was clinging to the trunk of the tree, shivering. He had seen something horrible. His face had turned dead white.

"What's wrong?" Miles asked.

"I saw it!" Augie insisted. "It was awful."

Miles peered into the jungle, wondering if Meat Hook and his men were going to charge them at any moment. "What did you see, Augie?"

Augie pointed toward the edge of the clearing. "There. It was over there. It came out of the jungle."

"What was it?"

Augie shook his head. "I—"

"Augie, you have to tell me what you saw," Miles insisted gently.

"A wolf!" Augie replied.

Miles frowned. "What?"

Len peered into the jungle. "You mean Joey Wolfe?"

"No," Augie said. "I saw a real wolf. It had red eyes and long ears. It came out over there. It looked right at me. But when I screamed, it ran back into the jungle."

Miles looked at Len. "Hayden, go see if there are any tracks over there."

"Me?" asked Len.

"This is stupid," Kirkland said. "That little wuss is lying. He didn't see anything."

Miles stood up. "Hayden, you stay with Augie. I'll have a look."

"Be careful," Len said.

Miles pushed his way into the undergrowth. Len went to Augie's side and put a hand on the kid's shoulder.

"I saw a wolf," Augie insisted. "It growled at me. It had a lot of white teeth."

"You didn't see anything!" Kirkland cried. "Stop lying to us right now, Augie. I mean it."

Len glared at the older boy. "Those scientists left behind Meat Hook and the other mutants. Why couldn't there be a wolf on this island?"

He tried to comfort Augie. The poor kid was still shaking. Had he really seen something in the jungle? Or had his imagination run wild, the way Len's own had that morning with the boats that turned out to be dolphins?

Miles burst out of the undergrowth. "I couldn't find any tracks. There's too much brush on the ground."

"I tell you, he didn't see anything," Kirkland railed. "There's no wolf on this island."

"But I saw it," Augie cried.

Len looked at Miles. "What do we do now?"

Kirkland bristled.

Miles folded his arms over his chest. "Ask Kirkland. He's the one in charge around here."

Kirkland pointed a finger at Miles. "You better shut up, punk."

Augie stood up. "*You* shut up, Kirkland. You can't boss Miles around. We don't have to do what you say. We can vote on who we want to be leader. I vote for Miles."

Len tried to restrain the smaller boy. "Augie, don't make it worse."

Kirkland glared at Miles. "See what you've started, prep? This is all your fault."

Miles sighed and unfolded his arms. "I don't want to be the leader, Kirkland. I just want to stay alive. How about you?"

Kirkland shook his head, looking away. He turned to Augie again. "Come on, kid. Did you really see a wolf?"

Augie nodded and stared at him with scared brown eyes.

"All right," Kirkland conceded. "Maybe he did see something. Who knows what those crazy scientists set loose on this island? There could be all kinds of monsters running around."

An abrupt silence settled in over the group. Shadows had crept through the jungle, and clouds had rolled up from the south. A dull rumble of thunder sounded in the distance.

"A storm," Miles said.

Kirkland looked up at the sky, which was barely visible through the vegetation overhead. "That was quick. We better head back to the compound before we're struck by lightning."

"I'm going back to the beach," Miles said. "I caught some crabs and dropped the sack when we ran."

Kirkland nodded toward the beach. "Go on,

then. Hayden, you take Augie back to the compound. I'll be there in a few minutes."

"What are you going to do, Kirkland?" Len asked.

Kirkland smiled. "I'm going to stay here and see if your wolf comes back. I won't be long."

Len nodded and took Augie's arm. "Come on, kid."

They started up the path, leaving Kirkland to watch the undergrowth.

Miles started toward the beach.

"Bookman!"

He turned back to face Kirkland. "Yeah?"

Kirkland looked away. "I don't mean to be a jerk. I mean—I just want us to get off this island alive. You handled yourself pretty good with those punks the last time. I trust you, and I want you to trust me."

"Sure, Kirkland. Whatever you say."

"Better hurry. The storm is coming."

"Don't hang out too long," Miles replied. "The wolf probably won't come back in the rain."

"You know, Bookman, sometimes you're too smart for your own good."

When Miles reached the beach, he could see the storm brewing to the south. Where had it come from? The sky had been clear just a half hour before. It was the beginning of the rainy season, and he knew there would be some rough weather ahead. The wind had grown stronger, whipping up a white froth on the surface of the Pacific.

Miles wondered if the warrior bandits might try to attack in the rain. Could they navigate the choppy water in the storm? He peered to the south as the dark clouds rose like a multiheaded monster from the angry sea.

He found the sack that held the crabs. He picked it up and started toward the jungle. The wind pushed at his back. A bolt of lightning ripped across the sky, followed by a deafening crack of thunder. It was going to be a bad storm. Miles hurried along the path.

When he got to the clearing, Kirkland was still there. The older boy was gawking at the undergrowth. His face had gone slack.

"What is it?" Miles asked.

Kirkland stammered, "I—it was—just like Augie said. I saw it with my own eyes."

"What?"

"A wolf," Kirkland replied. "It had long ears and white teeth. It came out and looked at me. Then it went back into the jungle."

"Come on," Miles said. "Let's get back to the compound."

Three

Joey Wolfe heard thunder as the cage hit the ground. His heart was pounding inside his chest. He was sure the bandits were going to kill him. The end was at hand.

Meat Hook glared at the Cherokee boy. "Open the door, Cannibal."

The bamboo gate swung open. Joey retreated to the back of the cage, but it was not far enough to escape from the fat man. Bullet Head reached in and pulled him out of the cage.

"I hate little fools like you," Bullet Head told him.

Joey wanted to fight back, but he knew he wouldn't have a chance against the mutants. More thunder resounded in the distance. Clouds had begun to roll over Lost Island.

Meat Hook reached toward Joey and put the point of his hook on the boy's nose. "You're a

31

stupid kid. Do you have any idea how stupid you are?"

Joey stared into the mutant's hideous face.

Cannibal stood beside Meat Hook. "Chief Worried Cat is not so brave now. Look at him. Trembling like a kitten."

Bullet Head chortled. "He's not a kitten. He's a chicken. A dirty little chicken."

"Go on," Joey said with false bravado. "Kill me now. Get it over with."

Meat Hook leered at him. "Do you think we're going to let you off that easy, stupid child? No, you'll pray for death before I'm finished with you. The worst is yet to come."

"We're gonna get your pal, too," Bullet Head chimed in.

"Vinnie's almost dead," Joey replied. "You can't hurt him anymore."

"Yes, we can," Meat Hook replied with a sly grin.

He drew the hook away from Joey's nose.

"What should we do with him?" the fat mutant asked.

Meat Hook gestured toward one of the palm and bamboo huts. "Put him in there until the storm blows over."

Bullet Head started to drag Joey toward the hut.

Meat Hook turned to Cannibal. "Get Toad Boy and Dog Face to put the other one in the hut with the Indian. Then have them come to my hut. We're going to do something about those brats on Apocalypse Island."

As he was dragged away, Joey was able to hear Meat Hook's last words. The others were alive, but he was still a prisoner. Bullet Head threw him into a dark hut.

"Don't try to escape, you little puke. I'll be watching you. We'll all be watching you."

"Bite it, fat boy."

Bullet Head pointed a finger at him. "When the day comes, you're mine. All mine."

"I can't wait, porky."

Bullet Head pulled a piece of cloth over the opening of the hut. Joey wondered if he could escape through it. He might be able to run, but where would he go? Meat Hook's men would be on him in a second.

The cloth flew away from the door. Two bandits with scarred and ugly faces brought Vinnie into the hut. They put Vinnie on the sand floor. One of them threw something at Joey.

"Feed these to your friend, chicken-boy."

They moved out again. Joey picked up a pill bottle from the sand. He could barely read the label in the shadows.

" 'Antibiotic penicillin tablets,' " he read. " 'Proteus Project Use Only.' "

Meat Hook wanted Vinnie to get stronger so he could torture him later. Joey opened the bottle. What if the pills were poison? He decided he would be doing Vinnie a favor even if they were. He lifted Vinnie's head.

The red-haired boy opened his eyes. "What—"

"Just take it," Joey replied. "It'll make you better."

Vinnie swallowed the tablet and closed his eyes again.

Joey leaned back, staring at the pill bottle. What was the Proteus Project? Did it have something to do with the place the mutants called Apocalypse Island? Kirkland and the others were there. Meat Hook had said so himself.

Joey listened to the gale wind blow over the hidden lagoon. The rain had not begun to fall yet. Then he heard Bullet Head talking outside the hut.

"Toad Boy, Meat Hook wants you and Dog Face in his hut right now. Don't keep him waiting."

"What for?"

"A mission," the fat man replied. "He's sending you to Apocalypse Island tonight, after it gets dark."

"Why?"

Bullet Head laughed. "To get the kids."

Toad Boy and Dog Face laughed too as they moved away in the wind.

Joey felt a chill down his spine. Meat Hook was launching another attack. He was going after them. And there was nothing Joey Wolfe could do to warn them.

Four

Miles and Kirkland hurried along the path. They were fleeing from the storm clouds that rode the hard wind from the south. Vines and treetops shook in the stiff gale. Large droplets of rain cascaded from the dark sky.

Kirkland broke into a run.

Miles ran after him. "Look out, Kirkland!"

He dived, hitting Kirkland and knocking the larger boy to the ground. Kirkland tumbled into the dirt, then jumped to his feet with his hands balled into fists. His eyes were wide.

"Bookman, you creep!"

Miles pointed to the path. "The man-trap. You almost stepped into it. The wooden spikes would have killed you."

Kirkland's hostile expression slackened into a dull frown. He looked at the pile of brush that covered one of the traps. They had set the spike-and-pit snares for Meat Hook's marauders. The traps had worked before. There were bandit bodies buried in the jungle to prove it.

Miles pointed up the path. "We better get back to the compound. And be careful of the other traps."

Kirkland nodded absently, fear and confusion showing on his face. He started to walk again, and Miles followed closely, watching him.

The path sloped upward, ending at the narrow stream that ran down from the higher elevations. Kirkland stopped for a moment. He stared up the slope as if he expected something to fall on him. Then he began to climb toward the compound. The path wasn't too steep. Miles came behind him, stepping carefully in the storm.

The rain was almost blinding. Lightning flashed overhead. Thunder rolled across the island as Miles and Kirkland came over the edge of the plateau. The scientists had built the compound on a flat ledge at the base of the mountains. The place was surrounded by mountains and rain forests.

Kirkland hesitated, staring at the lab building through the sheets of rain. He was spooked. Then he turned to look at the barracks adjacent to the lab building.

Meat Hook and the other criminals had been housed in the barracks while the scientists had been doing their experiments with the serum. The mutants had been spawned by the Proteus

Project. The boys had taken beds and blankets from the barracks, but they had not slept there —it was too scary.

"Kirkland! We'll drown in this rain if you don't hurry."

The older boy didn't seem to hear him.

Miles took his arm. "Come on. We've got to get inside."

As he led Kirkland toward the lab building, Miles took a look at the mountain behind the compound. He could barely see the peak through the driving rain. He had not been back to the secret cave in the mountain since he had flown the hang glider out of it for the battle. Miles wondered if there were more caves in the mountain.

The reception office of the lab was empty. The boys had straightened out the mess that had been left behind by the mutants' revolt. Bunks from the barracks served as their dormitory. They did all their cooking over a campfire outside or on the lab burners in the basement.

"Len!" Miles called.

The reply came from the lab in the cellar. "Down here, Bookman!"

Miles started to guide Kirkland toward the lab.

The older boy shrugged away. "No! Leave me alone. Get your hand off me."

Miles stepped back. He was afraid that Kirkland might snap. Maybe it would be best to leave him alone for a while. He started for the basement stairs.

Len and Augie were sitting beside the flame light of a lab burner.

"It's really coming down out there," Len said. "Bookman, you're soaked to the bone."

Miles sighed and sat down with them. "I'll dry out, but I'm not so sure about Kirkland."

Len squinted at his friend. "What's his problem?"

"He saw something he didn't like," Miles replied. "It blew his mind."

Len frowned. "What did he see?"

"Augie's wolf."

Augie stood up and pointed a finger at Miles. "I told you!" he said excitedly. "I said I saw a wolf, and I did."

Len pushed him down into his seat. "Take it easy, Augie." He looked at Miles again. "Kirkland said he saw a wolf?"

Miles nodded.

Len eased back onto a wooden lab stool. "Those research scientists left behind Meat Hook and the *Road Warrior* goons," he said. "What if there are all kinds of weird animals running around here? Your basic genetic mutoids. Killer monkeys or packs of wild tigers. This keeps getting more and more like a horror movie."

Augie frowned at Len. "What's a genetic mutoid?"

"Nothing," Len replied.

Miles looked at the younger boy. "Don't lie to him, Hayden. Augie, there could be more bad things on this island. You've got to be careful."

"I will," Augie replied. "But I want to get off this place. I don't want to stay here. I want to go home. I—"

His voice cracked as if he were ready to cry.

Len patted his shoulder. "Take it easy, kid. We're going to be all right. Don't worry."

Miles changed the subject. "Anybody hungry?"

Len nodded. "I am. What did you do with those crabs you caught this morning?"

"I dropped them in the storm," Miles replied. "Kirkland almost stepped into one of our traps. I had to knock him down to keep him from killing himself. I forgot about the crabs in the rain, and I'm sure not going back after them until this storm blows over."

Len shook his head. "I hope Kirkland doesn't lose it."

Miles stared at the flickering flame. "I'm worried, Hayden. He might freak out and try to hurt us. He was in that work camp before."

"So was I," Augie replied. "But we're not freaks, Miles. We're just like you and Len."

"Sorry," Miles replied.

They were quiet for a moment.

Len finally stood up. "I better open up the kitchen if we're going to eat."

"Say the magic word," Augie urged. "Go on, Len. Say it so the wall will open."

Len cleared his throat. "Okay, here goes. Proteus!"

They watched as one of the concrete walls began to move. Len had discovered the password by accident. Only his voice could activate the door that opened into the secret compartment. The others would say "Proteus" all day long, but the wall wouldn't budge. Len's voice was deeper than the other boys'. How was the door to know that he wasn't one of the scientists?

The wall slid open several feet, then stopped. Len moved through the portal. Miles got up and followed him into the chamber.

Shelves inside the compartment were covered with supplies the research scientists had left behind. Rows of five-gallon gasoline cans lined the wall. There was also freeze-dried food, canned food, rolls of thick rope, coils of barbed wire, hand tools, shovels, nails, axes.

Len grabbed three packages of freeze-dried beef stew and stepped out of the chamber with Miles.

When they were out again, Len spoke the code word. The door slid shut.

"We could always hide in there if the mutants come back," Miles said.

"You mean *when* they come back," Len replied.

Augie had an aluminum pot that they used

for cooking. "My stomach's starting to talk to me, Hayden."

"It'll be ready in a minute," Len replied. "Go get the jug of water we brought from the stream."

Augie walked across the basement to retrieve the jug of clear water. Len fixed the pot on a wire frame over the lab burner. He opened the packages and dumped the freeze-dried chunks into the pot. He added water and stirred up the mixture.

After they had eaten, Miles grabbed one of the gas lanterns they had found in the hidden chamber. "I need more light."

"I thought we were going to save the lamps for night," Len replied. "That fuel won't last forever."

"I want to study those records again."

"The log left by the researchers?"

Miles nodded. "I saw something yesterday that might help us. I want another look."

Augie yawned. "I'm tired. I'm going upstairs to take a nap."

Miles frowned. "Better leave Kirkland alone. He might still be in a bad mood, Augie."

Len walked to the front door of the lab. He gazed out into the puddled yard of the compound. The rain still fell in heavy sheets. Len watched it for a long time, wishing he was back home in New Hampshire. He looked over at

Miles, who was busy reading the abandoned records of the old Proteus Project.

"You get to the happy ending yet?" Len asked. "The part where we all live happily ever after?"

Miles looked up, rubbing his eyes. "I wish my glasses hadn't been destroyed. Reading gives me a headache."

"What did you find out?"

Miles looked at his friend. "I think there might be another lab somewhere on this island."

Len grimaced. "Get out of here! We've been up and down this whole end of the island. We haven't found anything besides this lab, a lot of jungle, and those mountains."

"I don't think it's on this end of the island," Miles replied. "Whoever wrote this keeps mentioning 'the hangar.' It might be some kind of storage facility on the other side of the mountain.

Len looked down at the log. "A hangar—isn't that where you store airplanes?"

Miles nodded. "Or other stuff. Who knows what could be there?"

"Does it say where this hangar is?"

"Not exactly," Miles replied. "But it could be past the mountain on the other end of the island. There might be a trail that we haven't found."

Len shook his head. "That's a dead end. We can't get over that mountain, can we?"

"Maybe if we got the glider working," Miles replied. "If we could repair the engine, then we could—"

They both looked up at the same time. They heard screaming coming from upstairs.

"The mutants!" Len cried.

Miles looked toward the hidden chamber. "Maybe we should hide."

But Augie appeared in the basement. "Bookman! Hayden! Come quick—Kirkland's in trouble."

They hurried upstairs behind the younger boy.

Kirkland was lying dead still in his bunk. He had a piece of rope on his chest—only the rope glistened with scales.

"It's a snake," Len cried. "A little snake."

"Shh!" Miles replied. "It's a krait."

Kirkland was sweating. "Get it off me!"

Miles held up his hands. "Don't move, Kirkland. The krait is one of the deadliest snakes in the world. If it bites you, you'll be dead in seconds!"

Five

By late afternoon, the storm had passed. Joey and Vinnie were taken back to the hanging cage. The bamboo cell was hoisted above ground again, giving Joey his dreaded view of the camp.

Joey fed Vinnie another one of the antibiotic tablets. So far, the medicine had had little effect on Vinnie's condition. He opened his eyes for a moment, then fell back into a deep sleep.

The air was fresh and cool after the rain. Joey leaned against the bars of the cage. When something tapped the bamboo, he turned to see a small sack on the end of a stick.

"Dinnertime," Cannibal said from below.

Joey took the sack from the end of the stick. He found smoked fish and bananas inside. There was also a skin of fresh water. He ate and drank as he continued to watch the camp.

Many of the bandits returned to their weap-

44

ons practice. They also went through martial arts exercises that were familiar to Joey from his own training. His father was an instructor in the military. Joey figured no one on the other island would stand a chance when the mutants reached full strength again.

Joey turned to watch Meat Hook's dwelling. Bullet Head came out and rang the gong. The two called Toad Boy and Dog Face ran to the sound of the gong. Their disfigured leader emerged to greet them. They rubbed against him like wild dogs in a pack.

Meat Hook led Toad Boy and Dog Face to the fire that Cannibal tended. They all drank from coconut shells. Whatever they were drinking seemed to whip them into a frenzy.

Joey cringed when the bandit leader spoke. His evil voice drifted up to the cage, and Joey could hear every hateful word.

"Are you prepared for your destruction, brothers?"

Toad Boy and Dog Face jumped up and down like monkeys. Meat Hook rubbed their heads like a benevolent master. They were ready to do his bidding.

"You will leave at once," Meat Hook went on. "You will reach Apocalypse Island by dark. Bring some bodies to me, or you will suffer a fate worse than death. Do not return until you have killed them."

Toad Boy and Dog Face ran toward their waiting craft. They launched the small sailboat into the lagoon. When the sail rose, they navigated the craft toward the channel that split the rocky cliff on the other side of the lagoon.

Meat Hook pointed his iron weapon at Joey. "All of you will die. A slow, horrible death."

The bandit leader turned and strode back toward his hut.

Joey slumped down in the cage. He had to find a way to get word to the other surviving boys.

Cannibal stirred below the cage. "Chief Worried Cat, you seem distraught this afternoon. What's wrong?"

Joey made a hostile gesture. "Shut up, you freak!"

Cannibal laughed and moved away. He walked to the edge of the lagoon and stared out over the water. Toad Boy and Dog Face were almost at the entrance of the hidden channel.

Tears rolled down Joey's cheeks. But he stopped crying when Cannibal began to feed the sea birds. The gulls and terns hovered in the air over Cannibal as he tossed bits of food into the sky.

Joey watched the birds for a long time before it hit him—a way to get his message to the others! It would take some doing, but it seemed to be the only way.

Joey just hoped he could pull it off before the bandit warriors killed Kirkland and the others.

Six

Len wiped the sweat from his brow. "It's been hours, and that snake still hasn't moved."

Miles watched the motionless krait coiled on Kirkland's chest. "That thing shouldn't even be here. It's native to Indonesia. Maybe those scientists brought it."

Kirkland lay still on his bunk. He kept his mouth shut on Miles's orders. Sweat soaked every inch of his body. But he was not going to give up.

"We've got to get it off him," Augie said.

Sweat poured down Len's face. "Why did it crawl on Kirkland?"

"It came in from the rain to get warm," Miles replied. "Kirkland was the first warm thing it found."

"It's sure hot in here now," Augie said. "I wish we had an air conditioner."

Miles looked at the younger boy. "That's it, Augie. You're a genius!"

Augie frowned. "Me?"

Miles raised his hands. "That thing came in here looking for heat, so if we want it to leave, we should make it cold."

"You're on to something, Bookman," Len rejoined.

"Grab something we can use as a fan," Miles said. "Hurry!"

They picked up flat pieces of debris from the piles they had made when they cleaned the lab.

"Fan the air," Miles told them. "Make it too cold for that crummy little reptile."

They began to beat the air, sending a cool breeze over Kirkland's chest.

"It's not working," Len said.

Miles watched the krait. "Wait."

Slowly, the snake came to life. It began to inch toward Kirkland's dripping face. The older boy had trouble staying still as it crawled over the bridge of his nose. He closed his eyes, trying not to flinch.

"It's working," Miles said. "Keep fanning."

The krait left Kirkland's face and crawled onto the pillow next to his head.

Len took a deep breath. "He's off!"

Augie clapped his hands. "You did it, Miles."

"We're not out of this yet," Miles replied. "Okay, Kirkland. You have to be quick."

"I'm ready," Kirkland replied.

"On the count of three. Ready. One—two—three!"

Kirkland rolled off the bunk. Miles immediately thrashed the pillow with a piece of wood. He beat the snake into a mass of bloody chunks.

Kirkland was trembling. "I hate this stinking place. I hate it a lot."

Len exhaled. "At least it's over."

Kirkland glared at him. "Is it?"

They were silent for a moment.

Kirkland started for the front door. "I've got to clean up and get a drink of water. My mouth is so dry, I'm spitting dirt."

He went outside and headed through the puddles toward the bubbling stream that ran down the incline.

Len looked at Miles. "You think he's lost it?"

Miles sighed. "I don't know. Come on, let's see if there are any more snakes in here."

Augie drew back. "I'm not looking. I hate snakes."

"Okay," Miles replied. "You go out and stay with Kirkland."

Augie flew out the front door like a hound after a rabbit.

"Let's do it," Miles said.

They began to beat around the room, trying to flush out more reptiles.

"Maybe that was the only one," Len said hopefully.

Miles turned over a piece of wrecked furniture. "It wasn't."

Another krait was coiled in a warm, hidden corner. Miles beat it to death. He must have hit it a hundred times.

Len grimaced at the bloody sight. "This just keeps getting worse. What's next? Fire-breathing dragons?"

"Keep searching," Miles urged.

But they did not find any more kraits in the room. Len sat down on the edge of his bunk, after he had checked it thoroughly.

In a few minutes, Kirkland came in with Augie in his tracks. "I owe you, Bookman," the older boy said. "You saved my life."

Miles shrugged. "You would have done the same for me."

Kirkland looked around. "Any more snakes in here?"

"Miles killed another one," Len replied. "But that was it."

Kirkland took a deep breath.

"Another day in paradise," Miles quipped. "It's time for me to take my watch on the beach."

"No!" Kirkland replied. "No sentry on the beach tonight. Everybody stays here and watches for snakes."

They spent the rest of the daylight hours removing the piles of debris from the lab reception area. Kirkland wanted the place bare. Len and Miles decided to humor him. After all, who wanted to wake up with a snake on his chest?

* * *

After dark, Miles brought up the lantern from the basement. They cooked more of the freeze-dried stew. Len added a can of carrots to stretch their dinner a bit.

When they were finished eating, things seemed calmer. They spent a restless night around the lantern, seeing snakes in every shadow, feeling kraits crawling under their feet. They had snakes in their minds. But there were no more reptiles or any other threatening animals.

They slept in short shifts, two at a time. Augie woke once, screaming from a nightmare. Everyone was relieved when the sun finally rose over the island.

Kirkland took charge again. "Roll out, dweebs. We're bringing that glider up the hill today. Let's see if we can get that engine running."

Len, Miles, and Augie hit the deck. They were glad to be awake, with no more snakes in their dreams to plague them.

"Keep your eyes open on the path," Kirkland commanded. "If you see anything, holler loud."

They moved carefully down the hill, following the stream. Kirkland stopped when they hit the path that led into the jungle. After a brief scan for snakes, he started along the trail. The others followed in his tracks.

"Looks like it's going to be a clear day," Miles offered.

But none of them echoed his false cheer. They kept plodding along behind Kirkland, and their wary eyes studied the shadows of the jungle.

"This was the place I saw the wolf," Augie said as they moved through the clearing with orange trees.

"Shut up," Kirkland told him.

They pushed on in silence.

When they came out of the jungle, Kirkland stopped and peered toward the beach. His eyes grew wide. The others gaped in the same direction.

"I don't believe it," Kirkland muttered.

Miles's face went slack. "No! It can't be."

Augie began to cry. "They were here last night! They could've killed us.'"

Len stared at the place in the shrubbery where the glider had been. "It's gone," he said. "Meat Hook's mutants stole our glider!"

Seven

Joey Wolfe worked hard all night. Using the switchblade from Vinnie's pocket, he stripped off long slats of bamboo from the floor of the cage. The darkness cloaked his activity, so the bandits couldn't see what he was doing.

By the time the sun rose over Lost Island, Joey had managed to free five pieces of bamboo. The slats were about six inches long and three inches wide. He hoped they would be big enough.

Vinnie stirred on the other side of the cage. He tried to sit up, then fell back again, holding his side.

Joey squinted at him. "You okay?"

"It still hurts," Vinnie replied with a groan. "But I don't feel as bad as I did yesterday."

Joey opened the pill bottle and took out a tablet. "Here, take this."

Vinnie stared at the pill. "What is it?"

"Penicillin."

"Where'd you get that?"

"The mutants," Joey replied.

Vinnie turned his head away. "Forget it. If those creeps gave it to you, it's probably poison."

"I've been giving them to you since yesterday," Joey replied. "That's why you're feeling better. Go on, take it."

Vinnie swallowed the pill. "How come those mutants want me to get better?"

"Why does a rancher want his steers to get fat?" Joey replied.

Vinnie moaned. "This bites it."

Joey leaned a little closer, holding his bamboo slats in hand. "Vinnie, Kirkland and some of the others are still alive. They made it to that other island. I think they're still there."

"Fat chance."

"No, I mean it. Somehow they defeated Meat Hook and his weirdos. Now the gang is looking for revenge. Meat Hook keeps talking about going back to the other island and killing them."

Vinnie lifted his head. "Man, that's not good news. What are those geeks going to do against these killers?"

"Don't you understand, Vinnie? These guys are human, even if they don't look it. If Kirkland could drive them off, maybe he can save us."

Vinnie lowered his head. "I doubt it."

Joey sighed. He was not about to let Vinnie get him down. He was going ahead with his plan. It had to work.

In the first hours of morning, the bandit camp was quiet. Meat Hook was still in his hut. Not even Cannibal had come out of his hut to tend his fire.

Joey went to work on the slats he had taken from the bottom of the cage. The knife point ticked on the bamboo. It was going to take him a while to carve the small letters on all five slats.

"What're you doing with my knife?" Vinnie asked.

"Trying to save our bacon," Joey replied.

His father had used that phrase. Joey found himself missing his father, which seemed ridiculous since they hated each other.

The first slat soon bore the message. He handed it to Vinnie. The words formed on Vinnie's lips as he read it: "Alive J W V P Danger."

"You could've left out the *danger* part," Vinnie offered. "If Kirkland and the others are still alive, they know all about the danger. You get what I'm saying?"

Joey nodded. "You're right. I'll leave it off the next ones. It'll be quicker that way."

Vinnie raised his head a little. "What if Kirkland is dead and it's just those prep dweebs? You think they'll come after us?"

"I don't care about that now," Joey replied. "I have to do this. It's the only thing I can think of."

"You think they're really alive on that other island?"

"Meat Hook and the boys are steamed," Joey said. "He told two of them to go kill the children on the other island. Why would he say that if the others were dead?"

Vinnie groaned. "A stupid piece of bamboo with some writing on it. How're you going to get that to the other island?"

Joey pointed toward the lagoon. "The tide goes in, the tide goes out. It's our only shot."

"You idiot. You can't throw that thing all the way to the lagoon. It must be fifty yards away."

Joey scowled at him. "Pelligrino, when they get the others, they're gonna kill us. Now shut your geek face."

Vinnie closed his eyes.

Joey kept at his task until he heard Cannibal stirring below him. The white-faced mutant stoked his fire. Joey turned his back to Cannibal, to continue his carving.

"Breakfast, Chief Worried Cat."

Joey froze. Could Cannibal see what he was doing? A stick tapped against the bars of the cage.

"We want you to be a fat little boy," Cannibal said. "You'll be on our table someday."

Joey almost dropped one of the bamboo slats as he took the sack through the bars. "Thanks for nothing," he said.

"I know you'll be nice and tender," Cannibal

56

replied. "Eat hearty. I wouldn't want you to lose any of that delectable flesh."

Joey kept his back to the bandit. "You ever think about suicide, you dirty geekazoid?"

Cannibal moved back to his fire. He was laughing. Everything evil and hateful was funny to him.

Joey reached into the sack. He found two smoked fish and some ripe bananas. He gave the bananas to Vinnie.

"Are you eating the fish?" Vinnie asked.

"No, I'm using it to save us."

Joey broke the fish into halves. He added them to the sack of fish he had saved from the day before. He hoped there would be enough.

"What're you doing?" Vinnie asked.

Joey didn't reply. He pulled out a piece of fish and shoved the slat through the center of the chunk. He molded the fish around the bamboo. Using a piece of his shoestring, he tied the fish securely to the slat.

Sweat broke over Joey's dark face. He would have to get it right the first time. The timing had to be perfect.

"Joey, you think—"

"Not now, Vinnie. Not now."

Joey watched the camp come to life. Meat Hook and Bullet Head called the others with the gong. They filed by Cannibal for their breakfast.

Meat Hook and Bullet Head went to the edge of the lagoon for a moment. They peered across the water. They were waiting for Toad Boy and Dog Face to return from their mission. Would they come back with dead bodies?

Meat Hook and Bullet Head got their food. They headed back to Meat Hook's large hut. The other bandits were busy eating.

Joey's heart began to pound. His moment was coming. He had to be careful.

Cannibal moved below him. Joey kept his eye on him.

Cannibal was gathering food scraps for his morning ritual. He took the scraps to the edge of the lagoon. The birds arrived on cue, hovering over him in the air, awaiting their handout.

Vinnie stirred a little. "What's going on?"

"Shut up, Vinnie!" he whispered.

"Hey, I—"

Joey pointed at him. "If you don't shut up, I'll kill you myself. Don't attract attention to this cage."

Joey looked out again. The move had to be quick. Cannibal's back was to the cage as he fed the squawking birds.

"All right," he muttered under his breath. "This is it."

He gazed upward. Soaring shapes filled the clear sky. The angle was bad. It would be a difficult throw, but it was the only way.

Joey grabbed one of the fish-covered slats of bamboo. He took a deep breath. His arm thrust between the bars of the cage.

If the bird didn't get the bait on the first

throw, the lump would fall to earth. Meat Hook's men would find the message, and Joey and Vinnie would go into the stewpot for sure.

Joey looked at the sea birds. "I hope you guys are hungry," he whispered.

A big gull flew over him. Joey launched his fish-covered projectile into the air. The gull swooped down at the bait and grabbed it with its yellow beak.

Joey raised his fist in the air. "Yeah!"

The gull lurched to one side. It dropped the bait to the sand below. The slat landed right next to Cannibal's fire.

Joey gaped at the fallen lump. His stomach did cartwheels. He could not find his breath inside his chest.

Cannibal turned away from the lagoon for a moment. His hollow eyes stared right at Joey.

"He saw it."

But then Cannibal turned back toward the lagoon. He continued to feed the birds. He hadn't seen a thing.

Suddenly something fluttered past the cage. A white gull dropped on top of the fish-laced piece of bamboo.

Joey grabbed the bars. "Do it! Do it, you air-rat," he whispered.

The gull lifted the bait in its beak. Its wings spread over the lagoon, the gull took off with the bait hanging from its maw.

"He did it, Vinnie," Joey said in a low voice.

"He's flying out over the lagoon. There! He let go of it."

Cannibal didn't seem to notice when the bait fell into the lagoon. Immediately, a dozen squawking sea fowl descended on the bait, tearing it away from the bamboo slat. A moment later one of the birds soared into the air. It carried the bamboo slat for a moment, then dropped it back into the water.

"I can see it, Vinnie. It's floating. It's floating."

Vinnie raised his head. "Awright, Wolfe!"

Grabbing another fishy slat, Joey thrust his arm out of the cage. He didn't have to throw it. A bold sea bird swooped down to snatch the lump from his hand. It carried the bait over the water and dropped it. Again the frantic flock descended on the lagoon. After a few minutes, the slat floated free.

"That's two," Joey said.

He repeated the process until the three other slats were floating in the lagoon. Joey was grinning. Then he noticed Cannibal leering up at the cage.

Joey's stomach began to hurt. "Oh, no."

"What?" Vinnie asked.

"I think the mutoid-boy saw me feeding the birds."

Cannibal glanced quickly toward the blue water. Joey wondered if he could see the slats as they twirled in the current.

Eight

The boys had gathered in the basement of the lab, shaken by the disappearance of the glider. Kirkland paced nervously back and forth. A trembling Augie sat between Len and Miles.

"They were here," Kirkland said. "Right down there on *our* beach. They stole that glider right out from under our noses."

Len folded his arms over his chest. "I wonder why they didn't come after us. We were all up here in one place. Why didn't they try to kill us?"

Miles looked up from the lab records on his lap. "They only brought one boat," he said. "And there were only two sets of footprints in the sand. Maybe they're still cautious about us. It could have been some kind of scouting party. Only two came ashore. They might still be here."

61

Kirkland glared at him. "Great. Just what we need—two madmen on top of us."

Miles shrugged. "I think they decided to take the hang glider as a second option. If we had been guarding it, they probably would've tried to hurt us. But when they found it unguarded, they decided to wait. They're probably out there right now stalking us."

"It worked out pretty good for them," Kirkland snorted. "Now we're stuck with no air power. We're dog meat."

"At least we're still alive," Miles offered. "And besides, I have a plan."

Kirkland pointed a finger at him. "You think you're so smart, you little grunt. Always lippin' off. Go on, hotshot. Tell me what we should do now. Let's hear what Mr. Know-It-All has to say."

Miles stood up so quickly that the computer sheets fell off his lap. "Kirkland, I'm getting tired of you getting so hostile. It doesn't help us when you blow your top."

"Yeah? What are you gonna do about it, grunt-boy?"

"I might just kick your stupid butt!" Miles challenged. "I'm not afraid of you."

Len tensed. For a moment, he thought Kirkland was going to jump on Miles. They were now locked in an intense staring match, but Miles would probably lose if things got violent. Len could not believe it when the older boy backed down.

Kirkland sat down and shook his head. "You've got guts, Bookman. I have to give you that much."

Miles shuddered. "Look here, Kirkland, when we drove off the mutants, you promised that we could trust you. You said so again yesterday. Are you backing off on that promise?"

"I'm scared!" Kirkland shouted. "Just like the rest of you. I'm afraid I'm gonna get you all killed! The way I got Vinnie and Joey killed! I want us to get out of this alive!"

"I'm just asking you to listen," Miles went on, knowing he had the upper hand.

Kirkland leaned back in his chair. "I'm listening," he said as if that was what he had been doing all along.

Len eased back into his seat. "Go on, Miles. Tell him."

Miles took the floor. "Okay, we know two things. First, Meat Hook wants to rock and roll on our faces. He wants revenge."

"Tell me something I don't know," Kirkland scoffed.

Miles glared at the older boy. "I thought you were going to listen."

"Yeah, yeah. Keep yapping."

Miles drew in a deep breath. "Second point. Meat Hook knows where we are. We're sitting ducks in this lab. The only thing that kept them from attacking us was the hang glider. Meat Hook sent a scouting party—maybe even a suicide squad—to make sure we couldn't attack

63

him from the air again. And he's probably getting ready right now to attack *us* from the air."

Kirkland grimaced. "So what? Like we don't know that."

"You want to fight him again?" Miles challenged.

Kirkland's rugged face turned red. "No, I don't want to fight 'em. But how do we get around it? Next time they'll bring everything they got. We'll be dead meat."

Miles pointed to the computer sheets. "These records keep mentioning a place called the hangar. I think there's another lab facility on this island."

"Yeah," Kirkland replied skeptically, "another mutant factory. With two-headed snakes and werewolves to rip out our throats."

"Or a better place to hide," Miles offered. "Who knows what we'll find on the other side of that mountain?"

"If we can get over it," Kirkland said. "You were up there once. Did you find a way to the other side?"

"No, but it could be there," Miles replied. "We could find a means of escape in the hangar. Or there might be somebody tending the place, who could help us get back to civilization. It could be so well hidden that Meat Hook and his men can't find it. The mutants may not even hunt for us if we head into the interior of the island. They might think we're dead."

"He's right," Len chimed in. "Anything is

better than staying here and taking it on the chin. Now that they have the hang glider, we can't fight back the way we did before."

Kirkland still did not seem to be convinced. "I can't buy it, Bookman. It seems like a wild-goose chase to me."

Miles straightened his body. "That's too bad, Kirkland."

"What do you mean?"

"If you don't go with us," Miles replied, "then we'll go by ourselves. Len and I can make it on our own. You can stay here with Augie and face the mutants by yourselves. Len and I will—"

Augie got out of his chair. "Forget it, Book-man. No way I'm staying here. If you and Hay-den leave, I'm going with you."

"Okay," Kirkland said with a sigh. "We'll do what Bookman says."

"Are you sure?" Miles asked.

Kirkland nodded. "Why not?"

Miles's face relaxed into a smile. "Good. Let's get ready. We start climbing the mountain in an hour."

"If you say so," Kirkland replied dubiously. "I just hope you geeks don't get us all killed."

Nine

Joey Wolfe kept his eyes on the mutant camp. He watched the birds float lazily over the blue lagoon. The bandits had been quiet all day. It worried him.

Toad Boy and Dog Face hadn't returned from their mission. They were still on the other island, probably trying to kill Kirkland and the other survivors. Where else would they be?

Vinnie raised his head. "Joey—"

"Chill out," Joey replied. "Everything's okay. You're still alive. Say a prayer, if you know one."

Vinnie lowered his head and sighed. "I feel better." He closed his eyes again.

Joey leaned back against the bamboo bars. He took a deep breath. Luck had been with him earlier in the day. Cannibal hadn't seemed to notice the messages floating in the water.

Joey wondered how long his good fortune would hold.

Vinnie suddenly propped himself up on his elbow. "Give me another one of those tablets."

Joey handed him another antibiotic tablet. "Get strong," he told Vinnie. "I'm not giving up until they lay me in the stewpot."

"That could be soon enough," the red-haired boy replied.

Vinnie seemed to be getting better. The wound had stopped oozing.

"I hope one of those messages got out of the bay," Vinnie said.

"You and me both. If we—"

The sound of the gong startled them.

Joey looked down to see Meat Hook and Bullet Head coming toward the cage. The other bandits fell in beside them. Joey thought they were coming to dinner—at least, until they stopped under the cage.

Meat Hook pointed at Joey. "You! Infidel! You have sinned! Now you must pay."

Bullet Head opened his right hand.

Joey's eyes widened. "No!"

Four of the bamboo slats fell into the sand.

How had they gotten the slats without Joey noticing?

"You are J. W.!" Bullet Head said. "Now you must suffer pain for what you have done."

Joey began to tremble.

Meat Hook nodded to Cannibal. "Lower the cage."

The bamboo cell inched toward the sand. The mutants crowded in for a better view of the torture. They wanted blood. Some of them were drooling at the thought of violence.

Meat Hook clapped his hands. "My instrument."

One of the bandits handed him a leather mass.

Meat Hook unrolled a long bullwhip. "This is what I use to play the music of torture and pain."

The other bandits gave a horrible laugh.

Bullet Head glared up at Joey. "This is going to be fun."

The cage hit the ground. The door opened. The bandit leader unfurled the lash. It wriggled in the afternoon sun, dancing in Meat Hook's hand like the long, dark tail of a poisonous viper.

Meat Hook lashed the Cherokee boy more than twenty times with his whip. Vinnie thought he could see bare bone in the center of the wounds.

Afterward, the mutants gave Vinnie a salve to put on Joey's wounds. Meat Hook was going to torture them forever. He would keep them on the brink of death, but he would never let them die.

Joey lived through the night. Vinnie sat up, gazing out toward the bandit camp. The mutants had not yet stirred for their morning ritual. There was still no sign of the two who had been sent to the other island. They were probably cutting off Kirkland's head to bring back to Meat Hook.

The stick tapped against the bamboo bars of the cage. Cannibal was offering the usual breakfast. Vinnie snatched the sack from the end of the pole.

"You're looking well, carrot-top," Cannibal said. "I like carrots in my stew." He laughed hideously and moved back to his fire.

Vinnie nudged Joey. The Cherokee boy opened his eyes. Vinnie gave him water and some of the bananas. Joey had to lie on his side to keep the whip marks from burning.

"Are you alive?" Vinnie asked.

Joey groaned. "I don't think so."

"I feel stronger," Vinnie replied. "Those pills are working. Here, you take one."

Joey shook his head. "Forget it."

Vinnie leaned closer. "Wolfe, one of your sticks may have gotten through. The geekazoids only found four of them. You threw out five."

Joey sighed. "Forget it. It's over for us."

The gong resounded through the bandit camp. They all came out of their huts for breakfast.

"Dead," Joey said in a faint voice. "We're all dead."

Ten

"It's the cave," Miles said. "The one where I found the hang glider."

Kirkland and Len stood next to Miles. They stared into the gaping mouth of the cavern. The climb had taken less than an hour. Even Augie had made it to the top of the trail without any trouble.

"What is it?" Augie asked. He peeked around Kirkland, and his eyes grew wider. "Wow! This is big. How'd it get here, Bookman?"

"Probably a side vent," Miles replied. "Lava flowed through here when this mountain was an active volcano."

Kirkland peered into the shadows. The cave opening faced west. The morning sun had not risen high enough to light the cavern inside.

"Pitch black in there," Kirkland said. "Break out the light, Bookman."

Miles displayed the lantern he had brought from the lab in a makeshift burlap sack.

They had tried to outfit as best they could for their exploration of the island. Their food, water, and a few tools were carried in crude burlap sacks. They had taken all their traveling gear from the Proteus chamber in the lab basement.

Kirkland had the flare gun tucked in his belt. The flare gun was their only weapon, and they also needed it for signaling in case a rescue plane flew over the island.

Miles lit the lantern with the plastic lighter that had been recovered from the plane wreck. "It's not bad in there, Kirkland. Just some shelves and the crate I tore apart when I found the hang glider."

Kirkland frowned. "Looks like a dead end to me. We came all the way up here for nothing."

"Maybe," Miles replied. "But you never know when we'll find something useful."

"Okay," Kirkland replied, drawing the flare gun from his belt. "Give me the lantern, Bookman."

Miles handed him the lantern. Kirkland lifted it and studied the entrance for a moment. Then he started into the cavern.

Len saw the light disappear around a bend in the hole. "Maybe those scientists dug this out themselves. I mean, they did have those mutants to do the work."

"No," Miles replied, "this is natural. I read about it in the log."

Len looked at the plateau in front of the cave. "Did you launch the glider from here?"

"Yes." Miles looked back. "You can see the beach and the compound from here. The water's clear. No Meat Hook."

In the hollow of the mountain, the yellow light illuminated the rock walls. "Okay," Kirkland called to the others. "Come on in. There's nothing much here. Looks like we wasted our time."

Len and Miles started into the cavern. Augie came behind them, hanging on to the back of Len's shirt.

The narrow corridor widened into a larger hollow. Barren shelves lined the walls. A dismantled crate lay on the floor.

"That's what the hang glider had been stored in," Miles said. "I found the bottles and the plastic container with it."

"The bottles you used to bomb the mutants?" Len asked.

"Yeah," Miles replied. "It was all together. I just had to bring up the gasoline."

Their voices echoed in the recess of the cave. The place was drafty and cool. It had a spooky feeling to it, as if there were something else hiding inside the dark walls.

Kirkland put the lantern on a shelf. "Nothing here, Bookman. We're stuck again."

Miles looked toward the mouth of the cave.

"There are other paths up here. We can try them. Maybe one of them leads to the other side of the mountain."

Kirkland shook his head. "This is dumb. We're wasting our time. We should be down there, digging in for the next attack."

"I'll stick with Miles," Len said quickly. "If we can hide, it's better than facing those goons head on."

"I still say it's stupid," Kirkland insisted.

Miles shrugged. "If you want to turn back, do it."

"Yeah," Augie echoed. "Just do it."

Miles eyed Kirkland. The older boy bristled a little. Was he going to start trouble?

"All right," Kirkland said finally. "Let's go ahead and walk those other trails. You won't be happy until you get us all killed, will you?"

A few hours later, they had come back to the coolness of the cave to rest in the shadows. Kirkland flopped down on to the ground. "This was another one of your stupid stunts, Bookman. Now we're back where we started."

Miles sat down on a boulder at the mouth of the cave. Augie sat beside him. Len looked out at the rain forest.

They were dragging after a hard day of searching in the sun. They had spent the rest of the morning and most of the afternoon walking the mountain trails. But every one had been a dead end. There did not seem to be a way to get to the other side of the mountain.

"We wasted a whole day," Kirkland said. "We could have been bracing for those mutants who came ashore."

Len's eyes grew wide. "Too late," he said. "Look."

Two figures were moving slowly through the undergrowth, on the other side of a narrow ravine about a hundred yards away. Meat Hook's men were in the jungle. A hideous face turned upward. The ugly man pointed toward the mountain.

Miles turned toward the cave. "Quick—inside!"

They all receded into the shadows of the cave. Miles tried to light the lantern, but it was out of fuel. He reached for one of the candles in his burlap sack. The flame flickered to life on the wick.

"Great," Kirkland said. "We're going to die in here."

Miles turned the candle toward the older boy. A sudden rush of air blew out the flame. Miles wheeled to face the rock wall.

"That draft came from back here," Miles said, "from the wall. I felt it on my neck."

Kirkland groaned. "Another one of your ideas."

Miles lit the candle again. He started toward the rear of the cavern. When he drew closer to the wall, a puff of air extinguished the flame.

74

"There's something back here," Miles said.

Len stared at the wall. "What are you on to, Bookman?"

Miles flicked on the plastic lighter. "Look." He turned toward the wall. The jet of the flame flickered in the draft.

"The air is coming from here!" Miles said.

"Right," Kirkland scoffed. "That's a wall of rock, you clown."

Miles torched the candle. He held it closer to the wall. The flame flickered and went out again.

Len saw it with his own eyes. "There's a seam in the rock!" he exclaimed.

"You're both crazy," Kirkland said. "We're dog meat unless we fight."

Augie moved closer to the rock. "I think Miles is right."

Miles ran his fingers along the crevice in the rock. "I can't find any . . . wait a minute."

Miles stepped back.

Len gawked at the wall of rock. "What's wrong?"

"Say the magic word," Miles told Len.

Kirkland grimaced. "Give me a break."

"Proteus," Len said.

The wall didn't move.

Miles tried it. "Proteus."

Nothing happened.

"Augie!"

"Proteus."

Len shook his head. "It's not working."

"I told you," Kirkland scoffed. "There's nothing in there. We have to make a stand against them."

Miles looked at Kirkland. "You say it."

"It's stupid, I tell you."

"Then make me wrong," Miles replied. "Say it, and you'll be the leader for the rest of time."

Kirkland grimaced. "Proteus. There, are you—"

The cave began to vibrate. Kirkland jumped to his feet. His voice had triggered another secret door. Part of the rock slid back. The opening was dark and narrow.

Miles started into the passageway. They all watched him disappear in the shadows. They stood there for a moment, feeling the cool breeze blowing through the secret door.

"Wow—it opened when I said the word," Kirkland said. "This is wild!"

Miles stuck his head through the opening again. "Look alive, campers! This is what we were looking for."

He disappeared back into the shadows. Len followed directly behind. Augie followed, and Kirkland came last. They started down a long, scary passageway.

"Weird," Kirkland muttered, his voice echoing through the hollow tunnel. "All this because I said 'Proteus.'"

Again the rumbling spread through the mountain. The door closed behind them. Kirkland said the password again, but the door did not reopen.

"Great going, brainless," Miles said. "Now we're stuck."

Kirkland scowled at him. "Quit your whining. We got a wall of rock between us and those mutants. We're safe now."

"Unless they know the password," Len offered.

Miles decided to make the best of it. "Come on, let's go see what I found."

They walked for ten minutes until they came to a dull glow at the end of the passageway. Cool air rushed through the tunnel. After a few moments, they emerged on a shelf of rock that overlooked the north side of the island.

The rest of the island stretched before them. Peaks of more volcanic mountains rose at the other end of the land mass. An entire valley below them was covered with thick rain forest. A sandy plateau sat beyond the jungle. The plateau seemed to separate the two ranges of mountains.

"Incredible!" Len said. "It doesn't seem real."

Augie's eyes grew wide. "It's so big. Look, more mountains."

Kirkland seemed impressed. "I don't believe it. The little tool was right."

Len said, "Kirkland, I'm glad you opened that door. This is better than the compound.

The mutants will never look for us here. They'll never find us."

"Don't bet on it," Kirkland replied.

Miles pointed toward the distant peaks. "I bet the hangar is on the other side of those mountains."

Kirkland glanced to his left. "Is there a way down?"

"That looks like a path," Miles replied, pointing to an opening in the brush.

They started down. The path was easy for a while, but they began to sweat in the tropical heat. Exotic birds flitted through the jungle. They could hear the cries of strange animals.

Miles turned a narrow bend. The path ended at a rocky outcropping.

"You screwed up, Bookman," Kirkland accused. "We're lost."

"We'll never get around that," Augie rejoined.

"Not *around*," Miles replied. "We'll go *over* it. There are handholds here. They were cut by someone."

Kirkland gestured toward the rock face. "Okay, hotshot. Go to it."

Without hesitation, Miles took hold and began to climb. He pulled himself over the crag. The others watched as he disappeared over the top.

Augie was on the verge of crying. "Bookman!"

"It's okay," Miles called. "There's a ledge

78

here. You can do it. Hurry up. It's not bad at all."

Kirkland looked at Len. "You're up, prep. If you make it over, I'll come with Augie on my back."

Len found a handhold in the rock and started to climb. The angle made him a little unsteady at first, but he finally came over the crag.

He dropped down next to Miles and gave him a high-five. "Made it, Bookman."

"All right, Hayden."

"Kirkland's going to bring Augie on his back," he said.

Miles frowned. "That's not a good idea. This angle is bad."

But it was too late. Len and Miles could already hear scuffling on the rock. Kirkland threw a leg over the crag.

"I'm making it," Kirkland grunted.

Augie was hanging on to his neck.

"Not so tight, Augie," Kirkland said. "I'm having trouble breathing."

Kirkland lost his balance for a moment. He slipped on the rock, just out of reach of Len and Miles. Suddenly Augie was hanging sideways from his neck. Kirkland's fingers grew white as he struggled to hang on.

"I'm going to fall!" Augie cried.

Miles reached for Augie's arm. "Hang on, we'll get you."

Augie struggled to find a toehold in the rocks.

With one hand he grabbed a vine that was shooting out from a crevice in the rocks.

"I think I'm okay," Augie cried.

But then the vine broke.

Len and Miles gaped as the younger boy plummeted toward the green carpet below.

Augie felt the air pushing against him as he fell toward the rain forest. One hand clung to his burlap sack as his arms and legs spread-eagled in the wind current that swept up the slope. The mountain passed in front of his eyes as a blur.

The green treetops rushed straight up at him. Then he hit a ceiling of tangled branches. The vines and twigs crackled beneath him as a thick carpet of vegetation slowed his fall. It felt as though thousands of needles were being jabbed into his body.

Augie grabbed a tangle of vines. The jungle sagged downward under his weight. He held on tightly, but the jungle gave way, and he was falling again.

His body crashed into another mesh of tree branches. He bounced back into the air when the branches surged upward. Augie flipped head over heels and tumbled toward the floor of the rain forest.

His eyes caught a bright reflection and his feet hit the glassy surface of a clear pool of water. The splash flew high into the air.

Augie was stunned for a moment. His body

sank deep into the pool. He opened his eyes to see colorful tropical fish in front of him.

The burlap sack was still in his hand. It was full of air, and its buoyancy floated Augie to the surface of the pool.

He sucked air into his lungs. He had to struggle to tread water. The fall had left him dazed.

Flailing at the water, he swam for the edge of the pool. Ribbons of green moss and brown roots hung over into the water. Augie grabbed the vegetation and pulled himself out of the pool. He lay belly-down on a carpet of green plants.

His body ached, but he was alive. He closed his eyes for a moment. When he opened them again, he opened his mouth to let out a desperate cry, but no sound came from his lips.

Red eyes loomed at him from the jungle. The face of a wolf came into focus. The animal's jaw was hanging low, revealing a sharp set of white teeth.

The wolf began to growl. It looked hungry.

Augie didn't have the strength to move as the animal started toward him.

Miles peered down into the ceiling of the rain forest. "Augie hit the trees and then he was gone."

"That's right," Kirkland said. "He's gone. He's dead."

Len felt a tightness in his chest. "Augie. I liked Augie. He was a good guy."

81

Kirkland glared at Len. "All right. Shut up."

He stared down at the forest again. Having almost fallen himself, he suddenly wanted to be off the mountain and on more level terrain. "Let's go, you clowns."

Len and Miles kept looking down.

"We should at least find him and bury him," Len said.

Kirkland grabbed the front of Len's shirt. "Didn't you hear what I said, freako? He's gone. Bye-bye. Dead meat. Dirt-nap city."

Len pushed Kirkland away. "How can you say things like that? That fall was horrible. Augie's dead."

Kirkland lifted his fist. "You little—"

Miles stepped between them. "Kirkland's right, Len. We can't lose it now. Augie's gone, but Meat Hook isn't."

"Augie's dead," Kirkland rejoined. "Yeah, it was horrible. But it doesn't change a thing."

Len lowered his head.

Miles looked toward the path. "We better get off this mountain before we end up like him."

The wolf's red eyes drew closer to Augie. The animal seemed to be limping as it came his way. Its growl turned into a slight whimper.

Augie sat up a little. "Don't hurt me."

The wolf stopped and lay down on the tropical carpet of green. The whimpering became louder.

"You're hurt," Augie said. "Aren't you, boy?"

The animal didn't seem threatening now. It was hurt and scared, like Augie. The animal's pain made Augie forget his own miseries.

Slowly, Augie stood up. "You hungry, boy?" he asked carefully in a low, calm voice.

The wolf whimpered. It had a ratty, matted coat. It looked skinny.

Augie still had his burlap sack. He reached in slowly and smoothly for a can of food. He found a tin of sardines that could be opened by the key on top of the can.

Augie quietly opened the tin and put it down for the wolf. "Here, boy. Come on, have something to eat."

But the wolf didn't eat. It lifted its legs into the air. Then Augie noticed the bloody paw.

"You are hurt!"

Augie started moving slowly toward the wolf. He carried the sardines with him. He put the tin by the wolf's snout.

"Go on, eat."

The animal sniffed the food. Its tongue came out. Then it began to lick the oil.

"Let me look at that paw," Augie said softly.

He started to grab the animal's wounded foot, but the wolf snarled and snapped at him. Augie jumped back. The wolf returned to licking the sardines.

Without touching the paw, Augie bent closer to look at it. A sharp piece of metal was lodged between the animal's foot pads.

"That looks bad, boy."

He knew what he had to do. He pushed the sardines closer to the wolf's head. When the animal started licking the can again, Augie reached quickly for the splinter instead of the foot.

His fingers closed around the shard of metal. The animal started to snap again, but when Augie pulled back, he had the splinter in his hand.

"Look, boy! It's out."

The wolf immediately righted his body. It ate the rest of the sardines without looking up. When the wolf had finished eating, it limped to the edge of the pool and began to drink.

"Guess I better get going," Augie said.

He turned to stare into the jungle. A narrow path seemed to wind through the tangled undergrowth. He started away from the pool. He had to find the others.

The path wasn't bad. But as Augie made his way through the forest, he heard the wolf following him. He stopped to look back. The animal was only a few yards behind him. His lip quivered as Augie moved toward him.

Augie's heart thudded at the thought of what the wolf could do to him if it attacked. He knelt. "Come on, boy. Don't be afraid. Come on, I won't hurt you. And you won't hurt me, I hope."

The wolf limped toward him, bobbing its snout in a friendly manner. It rubbed against Augie's fingers.

"See, I'm not going to hurt you. Yeah, you're a good boy." He rubbed the creature's head.

The wolf stayed by Augie's side as he traversed the trail through the jungle. A little while later, Augie was surprised when the wolf ran ahead of him. Its foot seemed to be better.

The red eyes kept looking back, as if beckoning Augie to follow.

"I'm coming, boy."

They walked together for a long time. Then Augie could hear the ocean roaring, and the wolf led him out of the jungle. They followed a trail between two rocky cliffs, finally emerging onto the edge of a sandy beach.

"Good boy," Augie said. "You brought me here. Now which way do we go? Wow, this is cool."

Augie bent to rub the wolf's head. The wolf licked his hand.

Augie looked to his left. The beach ended abruptly at a wall of rock. He couldn't go that way.

He looked to his right. The beach stretched as far as the eye could see. This was the only way to go.

For a few minutes, he watched the shadows creep over the beach, wondering what he should do now that he was separated from the others. It would be dark soon. But he wanted to walk as far as he could while there was still light left. Maybe he could find the others before nightfall.

He looked down at the wolf, who waited faithfully by his side. "You need a name, boy. I've got it—Commando. My dad used to call me his little commando."

Then they started up the beach.

Augie had not gone far before he saw two human figures walking toward him on the beach. He stopped. He had found Len and Miles.

Commando lowered his face and began to growl.

"It's okay, boy. They're our friends."

But when the two figures drew closer in the waning light, Augie saw that they were not Len and Miles.

Eleven

"Mail call, sir."

The ensign dropped the morning mail onto the desk of Lieutenant Branch Colgan. The Coast Guard pilot began to sort through the envelopes. He stopped when he got to the one with Senator Williams's return address in the corner.

Colgan was almost afraid to open it. But he had to read the news, good or bad. The lives of the lost kids might depend on it. He just hoped the senator had gotten him permission to fly into Omega quadrant.

He opened the envelope.

Colgan's face went slack as he read the letter. *Dear Lt. Colgan, While I owe you a debt of gratitude for your assistance in my rescue, I'm afraid that I cannot—*

Colgan looked up, grimacing. "No!"

Permission had been denied. Omega quadrant was still off limits. Not even the senator had enough power to get the okay.

The lieutenant would not be able to look for the downed C-47. Not officially or legally. Not in a Coast Guard plane.

What if he took the matter into his own hands? He could hire his own plane and go looking by himself. Still, he would be breaking the law. Omega quadrant was off limits to civilian flights as well as military flights. If he was caught, he would throw away all hope of helping the lost boys.

Colgan shook off the bad feeling in his gut. He tried to distract himself with the rest of the morning correspondence. On one envelope, he saw an unfamiliar name and return address: Sir Charles Bookman, British Embassy, Suva, Viti Levu, Fiji Islands. As Colgan began to open the letter, someone knocked on the door of his office.

"Come in."

The door opened. Commander Nickles entered the office. Lieutenant Colgan snapped to attention.

"As you were, Lieutenant."

Colgan relaxed. "Good morning, sir."

Nickles wasn't smiling. "Lieutenant, I hate to have to do this to you, but there's no easy way. I'll be straight with you. I'd want it that way if I was the one getting the news."

"What's wrong?" Colgan asked.

Nickles frowned and looked away. "You're

grounded, Lieutenant. Effective until I give further orders, you're no longer flying anything but a desk."

Colgan's eyes grew narrow. "But why? I have one of the best records in my squadron. I—"

"You went to Senator Williams, Lieutenant. You went over my head on the Omega quadrant thing. I told you to leave it alone."

"Sir, don't ground me. Flying is my whole life."

Nickles shook his head. "I tried to warn you. But the truth is, Colgan, the orders came from high up. So high, I don't even know who grounded you. I'm just the messenger. If it were up to me, I'd leave you in the air. But you stepped on some pretty big toes when you went to Senator Williams."

"But—"

"No buts, Lieutenant. You're grounded."

Nickles left in a hurry.

Colgan sat down at his desk. He was stunned. But what could he do? He was in the armed service of his country. He had to follow orders.

He looked down at his desk. The letter from Fiji was still there. He opened the envelope and started to read.

Sir Charles Bookman's son had been on the flight that had disappeared. Maybe Colgan did have one more chance to try to find those lost kids.

Twelve

The dark jungle hung over the boys. Len, Miles, and Kirkland hovered around the flames of a small fire. Nocturnal animals moved in the blackness beyond the yellow flames. The boys couldn't see the shapes, but they knew the animals were there.

Kirkland grunted. "Of all places, we have to camp in the middle of this jungle!"

Miles shrugged. "At least we're off the mountain. This was the only clearing we could find."

"Not much of a clearing," the older boy scoffed.

Kirkland's hands were busy at work on a long piece of tropical hardwood. He had torn the staff from a fallen tree. Now he was using a rock to shape the stick into a weapon.

Kirkland thrust the sharpened point into the flames of the fire. "I'm going to be ready for those geeks. Fire will make the tip hard."

Len stared out into the dark forest. "Look! Eyes!"

The luminous circles disappeared before the others could see them. Then something gave a low growl in the jungle, and the leaves rustled for a moment. Then a deadly silence settled in all around them.

"Augie's out there somewhere," Len said. "Those animals will find his body."

Kirkland lifted the point of the spear to Len's throat. "Shut up! I told you to shut up!"

Len pushed the spear away. "Bite it, Kirkland. I'm sick of you."

"You little—"

Miles lifted his hands. "Listen!"

A loud crackling resounded from the forest. Silence followed the echo. The fire began to die.

Miles threw more twigs onto the fire. "If this fire goes out, we're—"

A howl rose up in the darkness. Something had surely decided to spring an attack on the boys. There were a lot of them. They seemed to be coming from all directions.

Kirkland scrambled to his feet. He tried to draw the flare gun, but a canine shape had already leaped into the air. It was coming straight for Kirkland's throat with its teeth bared.

"Wolf!" Len cried.

Kirkland lifted the point of the spear in self-defense. The animal landed squarely on the end of the weapon. It squirmed as blood poured from its matted chest.

"You got him!" Miles cried.

Kirkland threw the body to the side, sliding it off the bloody spear. He could hear others nearby. There had to be a whole pack of them.

Miles looked closely at the dead animal. It was lean and muscular, with short grayish hair and a long snout. But it was obviously not a real wolf. It had the look of a dog whose ancestors had been living as strays for generations and had reverted back to wild form.

"They're wild dogs!" Miles said. "They aren't really wolves."

Miles reached down for a handful of twigs. He dipped them into the last flames of their campfire. The makeshift torch came to life.

"There are too many of them!" Len cried.

Another canine form sailed at them from the darkness. Kirkland drove the spear into its side. The animal yelped loudly, then fell, mortally wounded.

Two more hairy faces leered at Miles, snarling and growling from deep in their throats. Miles held the torch in front of him, jabbing at the white canine teeth. The hackles were raised on their backs and necks. But the wild dogs stayed just beyond the flow of the yellow flame, pacing and watching with fierce attention. They wouldn't attack with fire in their faces.

"The flare gun!" Len cried. "Use it!"

The torch died in Miles's hand. Both animals started forward. Miles didn't even have a club to fight them.

Suddenly a ball of fire streaked through the air. The animals in front of Miles seemed to explode into flames. They ran away, yelping as their fur burned to the skin. Kirkland had shot them with the flare gun.

"Good shot," Miles said.

Kirkland looked into the trees. "Part of the flare is still burning."

The bright orange glow lit the rain forest. They could see a path on one side and a pack of wild dogs circling them on the other.

"Move!" Kirkland cried.

They ran until they were no longer in the glow of the flare.

Miles pointed ahead. "Fire another one—it'll light the way."

Kirkland seemed to understand. He launched another fireball into the green undergrowth. The rain forest was so damp that not even the flares could set it afire. But the flaming ball showed the trail clearly ahead of them.

They continued to run. Miles led the way with Len, and Kirkland brought up the rear. One of the wild dogs circled around to their side. Kirkland didn't see it coming.

The wild dog hit Kirkland's shoulder, and he went down. The white teeth were all over him. He reached up to grab the animal's throat.

But the snout waved back and forth, and Kirkland couldn't find a grip.

Suddenly the dog gave a horrible yelp. Its body went limp. The animal rolled off Kirkland's chest.

Kirkland looked up at the bloody spear point. Miles had picked it up when Kirkland dropped it, and he had stuck the dog. He had saved Kirkland's life—again.

Len helped Kirkland to his feet. "Are you okay?"

Kirkland shoved Len away. Blood was dripping from Kirkland's face, but he managed to load the flare gun again.

"I'll get 'em," he muttered.

Kirkland fired another round at the wild dogs. The flame blazed a fiery path over their heads. They shrank back in fear.

"Run!" Kirkland shouted.

They bolted through the jungle again. After they ran a few hundred yards, the flare went out, leaving them in the darkness. Kirkland quickly made another shot to light the trail. They could hear the dogs on their heels. Kirkland reloaded the flare gun and fired again to drive the dogs back.

"We'll never get away!" Len cried.

"Keep moving!" Miles shouted.

They ran harder. The jungle seemed to be getting thinner. They could see stars overhead.

Miles was breathing erratically. "We're almost to the plain," he gasped.

Kirkland pushed them forward. "Don't stop —not if you want to stay alive. Those dogs haven't quit yet."

Miles knew the dogs had been brought by the researchers. Maybe the serum had turned the animals into monsters as well.

Another dog tried to attack. The barreling shape hurled at the boys out of the night. Kirkland wheeled to fire the flare gun.

The wild dog burst into flames as the ball of fire cut right through his chest. It fell onto the ground, squirming in a horrible shower of sparks.

Len looked back. "You must have thinned them out some."

Kirkland started forward. "Move it or lose it."

They had to keep running. But as they moved along the path, the trees disappeared over their heads. The sky was clear. Dried brush and low shrubs were the only vegetation.

They could still hear the dogs on their tails. The pack would cover the low ground with no trouble. They could stalk them better from every angle.

Kirkland turned to let another flare go in the dogs' direction. The pack was only a few hundred feet behind them. They seemed more determined than ever to kill the fleeing boys.

They ran out of the low brush, and the ground was suddenly flat and barren. But they could not stop to investigate. They had to find a way to hurt the pack. Even the flare gun seemed to have limited effect upon the wild dogs.

After they ran several hundred yards, they stopped to catch their breaths. Their chests ached. Kirkland's face was still bleeding from the dog bites.

"We're on the flatland," Miles said. "The ground is hard."

Kirkland gazed behind them. "It will be bloody if those hounds get us."

Len stared into the shadows. "I don't hear them anymore."

Kirkland fired another flare into the sky. The burning light revealed the pack of wild dogs at the edge of the low brush. They were no longer running. Some of them were sitting, while others were lying down.

"They've stopped," Len said.

Miles peered at the glowing red eyes. "Maybe we scared them. They're finally afraid of us."

Kirkland turned to gaze out over the flat, dark, unknown plain. "Maybe there's something out there that scares them even more," he said.

They stood on the flat ground, watching the pack for a long time. The wild dogs wouldn't venture out onto the plain. But they wouldn't run away, either.

"They're trying to wait us out," Kirkland

said. "They want us, but they don't want us bad enough to chase us out here."

Miles turned, staring to the north. He could see very little on this moonless night. Dark shapes—probably the other mountains—loomed against the vague light of the stars.

Kirkland looked at him. "Got any ideas, Einstein?"

Miles sighed. "If we keep going, we'll reach the other end of the island. That's where I want to be."

Kirkland shuddered. "Those dogs are scared to come out here. What's waiting for us out there?"

"I don't know," Miles said. "Maybe something worse. Or maybe something that will save us."

"Let's keep going," Len offered.

Kirkland shook his head. "Wild dogs. Mutants on our tails. What next? Flying crocodiles?"

"You can go back anytime," Miles said.

Kirkland peered into the northern shadows. "No, I don't want to go back. Let's move."

They began walking across the flat, hard ground. After a while, they looked back to see if the dogs were following. But the pack had not ventured onto the plateau.

"What are those mutts afraid of?" Kirkland muttered.

But Len and Miles didn't reply. They were

numb. There was nothing for them to do but trudge forward into the unknown darkness.

They had been walking for hours. Dawn had broken, and the sun was now high over the island. Wavy lines of heat rose from the barren stretches of the flatland. The air seemed thin. It was almost like a desert.

Miles couldn't move another step. Kirkland also staggered to a halt. His eyes drooped and his face sagged. They hadn't slept at all the night before.

Len dropped to one knee. "Too hot. Water."

They drank sparingly from their supply, but the water was almost gone. And the mountains in the distance didn't seem to be getting any closer.

"I'm dead," Kirkland moaned. "But there's no place to get away from this heat."

Miles was sweating from every pore in his body. "Wait a minute."

Kirkland grimaced. "What now, geek-brain?"

Miles held up his burlap sack. "Let's undo the seams of our bags," he said. "We'll piece them together to make a tent."

Kirkland looked away. "Forget it."

Miles started to work. "It may be crude, but it's better than dying."

Len was pleased. "Good thinking, Book-man."

In a half hour, they had erected a rough but

effective source of shade. Kirkland's spear propped up the tent in the middle. The boys had to hold the sides to keep the shelter balanced.

They sat there in silence, back to back, and took a short nap while the sun got lower in the sky. When the late afternoon heat began to lessen, they awakened and came out from under the tent.

"How do we carry our stuff?" Kirkland asked, rubbing his eyes.

"Roll the burlap together," Miles replied. "Put our gear inside."

When they were ready to travel again, Kirkland looked to the west. The sun had fallen behind the rocky escarpment that ran on that side of the island. It would be night soon.

"We could go that way," Kirkland said, pointing west. "There might be water in those rocks."

Miles peered to the north. "I'm making for the mountains."

"Oh, you're the leader now!" Kirkland scoffed.

Miles glared at the older boy. "It's every man for himself now, Kirkland. Haven't you figured that out yet?"

Kirkland bristled. "I'm gonna body-slam you, dork!"

"I'm heading for the mountains," Miles said. "If you want to come along, you're welcome."

Miles started north.

Len fell in beside him. "Don't get lost, Kirkland," he called over his shoulder.

Kirkland grimaced, but he picked up his things and went with them.

They walked until dusk. They finished the rest of the water, each of them taking one final swallow. If they were going to survive, there had to be water in the mountains. And they had to get to it soon.

Darkness eased over the plain. They kept going, their weary, aching legs stumbling on the hard earth. They kept moving, minute after minute, plodding in the darkness like dead men who had come back to life.

Kirkland was the first one to give up on the night walk. He flopped onto the ground. Len sat down beside him.

Miles peered toward the dark shapes that rose against the stars. How much farther would they have to go to reach the mountains? All of a sudden it didn't matter. He only wanted to rest.

Miles stretched out on the ground. "I need to sleep. Start again later. Sleep now."

Len and Kirkland didn't hear him. They were already out. Kirkland snored loudly.

Miles closed his eyes. He slept for a long time, dreaming of the cool, green playing fields at school. When he awoke, the sun was high and Len was screaming bloody murder.

Thirteen

"Bookman!" Len cried. "You've got to see it!"

Miles raised his head. Kirkland was gone. Len was running toward him.

"It's great!" Len cried. "You've got to see!"

Miles sat up. He peered toward the mountain peaks that rose over him. The slopes glistened in the sunlight.

"We made it!" Len cried. "We were here last night, but we didn't even know it."

Miles couldn't believe it. "We really made it!"

Len helped Miles to his feet.

"Kirkland and I just found it," Len went on. "We woke up a few minutes ago. I heard the water."

Miles glanced upward. He could see a rainbow cast by a waterfall in the distance. A lush green tropical oasis bordered the rim of the arid salt flat.

101

"There's food here, too," Len said eagerly. "We did it, Bookman! You were right all along."

They ran for the pool of clear water. A lava rock basin caught the water that fell from the slopes above. Miles dived headfirst into the basin. The cool water revived him.

He bobbed up next to Kirkland. "We made it, Neil."

Kirkland just rolled his eyes and swam away.

Miles drank until he was quenched. He swam to the edge of the pool and pulled himself onto a carpet of tropical moss.

Len was there, stacking bananas and oranges in two piles. "You were right, Bookman. Those scientists *were* on this end of the island. They must've planted all of these fruit trees."

Miles grabbed a ripe banana. "Wild. The trees seem to be at the same stages of maturity as the others back by the lab. We're getting closer, Len."

"Closer to what?" Kirkland challenged.

"I'll tell you after I eat," Miles replied. He filled his belly, then drank again. His strength was starting to return.

Len also felt better. "What now, Bookman?"

Miles lifted his eyes to the volcanic slopes of brown rock. "Those papers in the lab said the hangar is situated in a valley between mountains. It could be on the other side of this mountain."

Kirkland shook his head. "You never quit, do you, butt-head?"

Miles ignored Kirkland's continued slights. "I have to climb up there, Hayden."

Len frowned. "Maybe there's an easier way to look for this place."

"There's no hangar," Kirkland insisted.

Miles stood up. "I'm going up there to find a route. Len, why don't you and Kirkland look for a route on the ground?"

"Now he's making sense," Kirkland replied.

Len frowned at Miles. "You're leaving me alone with the Thing?"

"I heard that," Kirkland snapped.

Len turned to face him. "Who cares?"

"I'll pound you, Hayden!"

"Go on, big man. I might just pound you back!"

"Hey!" Miles cried. "Take a chill pill. We'll do it my way. Len and Kirkland take the low ground, and I'll climb."

Len shook his head. "Aw, don't—"

"Forget it," Kirkland said. "Let the little creep climb the mountain. He wants to be a hero. Let him die trying."

For the rest of the morning, Miles struggled up the mountain. The vegetation helped him part of the way, but when the clinging vines and shrubs disappeared, he had to climb using handholds in the rock.

The going was rough. But he kept moving. He took the mountain an inch at a time.

After a while, he stopped and looked down.

He had lost sight of Len and Kirkland. They had disappeared.

Miles gazed upward. He thought he could see the peak of the slope. Just a little bit farther. He grunted and started to climb again.

As the sun rose higher in the sky, Miles heaved himself over the rim of a flat ledge. He had made it. But he had to rest.

Sitting on the ledge, Miles peered down into a golden valley. His eyes grew wide. There it was!

A smooth, round dome reflected the midday light. The structure was huge. It rested in a valley between two mountains, like the egg of a giant bird.

"The hangar!" Miles cried joyfully.

But he didn't stay happy for long. Something swooped by his head. At first, he thought a sea bird had buzzed him.

He raised his eyes to the sky. Blue silk wings fluttered against the blue backdrop of the sky. Miles was paralyzed.

"The hang glider!"

The blue wings caught a current of air, then swept back toward him. Miles could see the evil face of Meat Hook's assassin. The mutants were finally launching another attack.

Toad Boy hung in the harness of the glider. The motor had been removed, but the craft soared high on the currents of air that whipped around the island. The blue-winged angel of death swooped down toward the ledge where Miles stood trembling. He gaped wide-eyed at the attacking bandit.

As the glider drew nearer, Miles saw a flash of polished steel. Toad Boy swung a long-bladed saber as he passed over Miles's head. Miles barely ducked under the shining weapon in time.

The blue wings banked to the right, swinging over the dome of the hangar. For a moment, Miles thought the glider was going to crash into the dome. But Toad Boy steered the craft back into the air currents. The glider rose again toward the ledge.

Miles was frozen on the mountain. He glanced to his left and right. There was no place to go unless he wanted to climb back down the steep slope.

His head snapped up. The glider was soaring straight toward him. Meat Hook's minion gawked at Miles with the hateful stare of a satanic demon.

Toad Boy swung low. Miles dodged the bandit's grasping hand at the last moment by dropping to his stomach. But something caught his shirt. He was dragged across the ledge to the edge of the cliff by the wing of the hang glider.

Miles grabbed the rim of the ledge. The glider tore away the back of his shirt. He hung there, his legs dangling in the reflection of the dome.

He had to get back onto the ledge before he

fell. His arms were burning. He tried to pull himself upward.

The shadow of the glider appeared over him. Toad Boy swooped out of the sky once again. Splotches of sunlight reflected from the saber.

The blade cut through the air. Miles ducked his head. He felt the sting on the back of his hand. The glider sailed by, heading for the desert air currents.

Blood trickled from a nick in his hand. At least Miles still had all his fingers. And his head.

A surge of fear gave him the strength to climb back onto the ledge. He took a deep breath. Adrenaline coursed through his body. For a moment, he forgot the pain.

He gazed into the sky. The blue glider caught a hot palm of air from the flatlands. Toad Boy turned the craft lazily toward the mountain. He was on the attack again.

Miles searched for a weapon. The ledge was bare. There was not even a loose rock to throw at the mutant.

The glider leveled off, coming straight for the ledge. Miles crouched down. It was all over. He didn't have a chance.

But at the last moment the bandit warrior took the glider higher over the mountain. Something sparkled in his hand. The blue wings cast a shadow on Miles's face.

A round, burning object fell from the sky. The bomb crashed on the rocks in front of Miles. Flames spread toward him.

Heat licked his face. There was no place to escape unless he could climb down. He was a sitting duck from any angle.

He edged along the rim of the ledge toward the north. The glider had already turned, and Toad Boy dropped another bomb. Flames now engulfed both sides of the peak.

"You ugly mutant!" Miles cried.

Fire welled up around Miles. He would be baked to death. He had to get off the ledge.

Suddenly the glider came back at him. Toad Boy could not resist one more attempt to grab Miles.

Miles stared intently as the glider came on. In a flash, he had an idea. It was his only chance.

The glider rushed over the ledge. Miles ducked Toad Boy's clutches just in the nick of time. Then, just as the hang glider swept past, he sprang up, grabbed Toad Boy's legs, and hung on. Toad Boy's eyes grew wide.

Miles sailed off the ledge. The glider sank with the extra weight of Miles's body. They flew over the bright glow of the dome.

Toad Boy reached back with the saber and tried to knock Miles off the glider. But the angle was bad. Toad Boy couldn't cut him.

Miles bit into the mutant's leg. Toad Boy screamed like a mad badger and dropped his saber.

Miles bit him again. He dangled from the glider with his teeth locked in the bandit's

107

flesh. The craft swung out over the blue water of the Pacific.

A bright beach stretched below them. Miles stopped biting. He saw sand and the water.

Suddenly one of the wings on the glider collapsed. The extra weight had done it. The craft was not made for two people.

They tumbled toward the earth, heading for a crash landing on the beach.

Len and Kirkland looked up when they heard the explosion on the mountain. A fireball rose into the sky. The rock face was in flames.

"Miles!" Len cried.

Kirkland gawked at the sky. "Look—the glider!"

They watched Miles battle the mutant.

Len pointed toward the sky. "They're both flying!" he cried.

Kirkland grimaced. "They're both going to crash on the beach if—no! What does Bookman think he's doing?"

As the glider fell, Miles let go of Toad Boy's legs. His trajectory carried him toward the blue water. He landed feet-first in the sea.

The glider crashed onto the sand. Len and Kirkland ran toward the wreck. A short, ugly man was squirming from beneath the blue silk.

Kirkland stopped dead. "Mutant at twelve o'clock."

Len almost stumbled into the sand. "Whoa! He's ugly."

Toad Boy gawked at them. He was unshaven and he had a mean look in his eyes. On his right arm, there was a tattoo of an evil-looking toad. He growled at them like a cornered animal.

Kirkland lifted his spear. "It's curtains for you, geekazoid!"

But Toad Boy was too quick. He lunged to his left, running for the jungle growth that lined the beach. Kirkland started after him, but the bandit was too fast.

"Let him go," Len said. "We've got to help Miles."

They turned back toward the water. Miles's head bobbed in the waves. Len dived into the surf. He swam out and dragged Miles back to shore.

"Is he alive?" Kirkland asked, gazing down at Miles.

"I think so," Len replied. "He's breathing."

Miles opened his eyes. "What happened?"

"You fell," Len replied with a nervous smile on his face. "You were riding on the glider with that mutant."

Miles sat up quickly. "Help me up," Miles said. "We've got to find a place to hide."

They lifted him to his feet. His legs were weak, and he had to lean against Len to get his balance.

"We aren't hiding anywhere," Kirkland replied. "Hayden and I found something to escape with. Look!"

Miles lifted his eyes. He spotted a small sail-boat pulled up on the beach.

"That mutant boat is our ticket out of here," Kirkland said.

Miles shook his head. "No. At least, not right now."

Kirkland frowned. "Are you nuts? Let's go before the whole fleet sails in."

"That's just it," Miles replied. "We'd be in worse shape on the water. What if they surrounded us? At least if we stay on the island, we can find a place to hide."

Kirkland kicked the sand. "I'm tired of you giving the orders, Bookman. You're not telling me what to do anymore."

"Miles has a point," Len said. "If we try to leave now, Meat Hook's gang might see us on the water."

"We could go at night," Kirkland said. "They wouldn't see us then."

Miles nodded, smiling. "Excellent idea, Kirkland."

"What?"

"We stay here and guard the boat," Miles replied. "Go up in the palm forest. Wait until it gets dark."

"But those mutants are in there," the older boy insisted.

Miles nodded toward the sea. "The mutants are out there, too. Take your pick. We have to wait. It's our only chance. Come on, Hayden."

Len started to guide Miles toward the jungle.

110

"Forget about him, Bookman. He's not going to listen."

"We better find a place to dig in," Miles went on. "It won't be long until dark. A few hours."

They kept walking in the sand. Kirkland lagged behind.

"I was flying," Miles said. "Did you see that?"

"I saw," Len replied.

"I saw the hangar, too," Miles went on. "I guess that doesn't matter now that we're leaving tonight."

"No," Len said. "It doesn't."

Kirkland called at them. "Hey!"

Len and Miles kept walking.

"This is stupid," Kirkland called. "Hey, wait up!"

Long shadows crept over the north end of the island. Len, Miles, and Kirkland had been hiding in the jungle all afternoon. Miles had been telling them about the hangar he had seen from the ledge. Kirkland didn't seem to believe him.

The boys could see the beach from their vantage point in the jungle. So far, neither one of the mutants had returned to claim the boat.

"I wonder where he is?" Len asked.

"Probably signaling the big kahuna back at the other island," Kirkland said. "This one was sent to get a lock on us."

"Meat Hook is afraid," Miles rejoined.

"Tigers aren't afraid of rabbits," Kirkland

111

said. "You can bet the rest of those creeps are on the way."

They kept peering toward the boat.

"It's almost time," Kirkland said.

Miles gazed out at the dark horizon. "We have to sail east. Maybe we can make it to a shipping lane or a civilized island."

Len clung to the big burlap sack. "I packed bananas and oranges this morning. The water bottles are full from the spring."

The last rays of the sun finally subsided.

"Okay," Kirkland said, "let's do it."

They left their hiding place and started through the jungle. The boat lay on the beach ahead of them. It would be harder to rig the mast in the dark, but it was still their best chance to escape.

"All clear," Miles said.

Len was sweating in the cool evening air. "We'll have to push it out beyond the waves. I hope there are oars inside."

"Shut up," Kirkland replied. "Just move!"

Carefully they hurried forward in the shadows. The sand squeaked as they made their way down the beach.

As they neared the clear stretch of shoreline, a sudden beam of light swung into their eyes, blinding them for a moment. Two figures eased out from among the palm trees.

Toad Boy and Dog Face moved toward them. Toad Boy had a crossbow. His finger was on the trigger mechanism.

A hideous voice rose above the sound of the surf. "Which one of you wants to die first?"

The crossbow was pointed at Kirkland's chest.

"Take the big one first," Dog Face whined. "Kill him before he causes trouble."

"Take careful aim," Toad Boy rasped. "Carve out his heart. We'll bring his meat to Cannibal."

Dog Face clapped his hands. "It's over, boys."

"Meat Hook will be so proud of us!"

"Run!" Miles cried. He turned away from the light, but his eyes had been blinded. He tripped into the sand, knowing that he would be shot.

But suddenly the spotlight lifted off them.

Dog Face swung the beam into the jungle. Toad Boy whirled toward the undergrowth with the crossbow. He fired an aluminum arrow into the trees.

But it was too late for the mutants. A dark shape had already sprung silently into the air. Toad Boy fell when the wild dog hit him.

Confusion rose on the darkened beach. Len was not sure which way to go. Kirkland hesitated, watching the dog chew on Toad Boy.

Miles lay in the sand. He thought the pack had found them. But he could hear only the one animal in the darkness.

Dog Face shone the beam of light on his partner. The dog was all over Toad Boy. Dog Face reached for Toad Boy's crossbow.

Kirkland cried, "Don't let him get the weapon!"

He took a step toward Dog Face. Then three more figures rushed from the jungle—human figures. And they beat on Dog Face.

Dog Face dropped the light. He squirmed away from his attackers and fled back into the shadows. One of the new intruders picked up the light. Another one grabbed the crossbow.

Kirkland stepped back. "Don't shoot!"

The wild dog jumped off Toad Boy. A loud twang sounded as the crossbow erupted. Toad Boy's head was pinned to the sand. The body lay twitching helplessly.

Kirkland gaped at the dying mutant. "Wow."

Finally Toad Boy's muscular body relaxed. He seemed asleep, except for the puddle of blood that formed in the sand around his head. The evil-looking toad, tattooed on his right arm, stared up at the boys.

Len was frozen by the spectacle. "I don't believe it." The scene sickened him. He turned away and tried not to get sick.

Miles got to his feet, taking a step toward the newcomers. "Hey, where did you . . ."

The dog ducked its head low, growling at Miles.

"Commando! No!"

Miles was astonished when the dog backed off at the command.

Augie stepped into the circle of light.

Kirkland gaped at him. "Augie! You fell off the mountain!"

"Yeah, but I didn't die," Augie replied. "I fell into a pool. Look who else I found."

Two boys stepped up next to Augie. One was a skinny, long-haired kid. The other was shorter than Augie and he had a punky haircut that had grown out some. The three of them looked ragged but healthy.

"Hi, Kirkland," the small one said. "It's me, D.J. Remember? We were at the work camp together."

"He remembers," the taller boy said.

Kirkland was trembling. "Cruiser, is that you?"

"Yeah," the boy replied. "We survived the crash. Only we got separated. We woke up on this island. Wild, huh?"

Cruiser was fourteen years old. D.J. was twelve. They had been on the plane from Fiji with the others.

"I found them on the beach," Augie said. "They were exploring, just like us. I couldn't believe it."

Cruiser pointed at Miles. "We saw you fighting that mutant on the glider. We wanted to help."

"Took us all day to get here," Augie told them. "Looks like we made it just in time. Are any more of those mutants here?"

"I don't know," Kirkland replied. "Cruiser, how'd you and D.J. stay alive all this time?"

"We found that spring on the other side of the jungle," Cruiser replied. "At the base of the mountain, where all the fruit trees are growing."

Miles leaned close to Len. "More delinquents," he whispered. "Just what we need."

"Three more against Meat Hook," Len replied.

Kirkland was glaring at Commando. "Where'd you find the mutt, Augie? We were almost killed by a pack just like him."

"I didn't find Commando," Augie replied. "He found me. And the three of us found this, Kirkland. It was floating in the surf."

Augie reached into his shirt. He pulled out something long and flat. He handed the sliver of bamboo to Kirkland.

He read the message on the slat of bamboo.

Alive J W V P Danger

"Joey and Vinnie!" Kirkland cried.

Miles leaned over to read the slat.

"I thought so," Augie replied. "We've got to save them."

Kirkland nodded. "I know how to do it. We've got the boat there. We can pull it off."

Miles cleared his throat. "That might not be such a good idea, Kirkland."

The older boy glared at him. "No? What would *you* do?"

"We can sail the boat into one of the shipping lanes," Miles replied. "We still have the flare

116

gun. We can send somebody back for Joey and Vinnie after we're rescued."

"Chicken!" Cruiser said, making a clucking noise.

"No," Miles went on. "I'm not afraid. I'm just trying to be smart. If we go against those mutants again, we'll all be killed."

"We did it once," Kirkland said. "We freed you and Hayden. We can rescue Joey and Vinnie."

"*If* they're still alive," Len offered. "We don't know when that message was sent."

Cruiser laughed. "Another chicken."

"Use your heads," Miles replied. "If we're all dead, what good will that do Vinnie and Joey? This way, at least some of us survive and the others have a chance of being rescued."

"I'm not leaving them on that island," Kirkland said. "We're going in. You want to vote on it?"

Miles pointed to the jungle. "What about the one who escaped? He could warn them."

Kirkland ignored Miles and looked at the others. "All in favor of going after Joey and Vinnie raise your hands."

The newcomers sided with Kirkland. Len and Miles were voted down, four to two.

"Come on," Kirkland said. "We're leaving for the other island as soon as we can get that boat in the water."

"Too bad for us," Miles said, shaking his head.

Fourteen

The water lapped against the hull of the sailboat. Miles was sitting at the tiller, steering the small vessel. Kirkland knew Miles was the best sailor, so he put him in charge of navigation. A sliver of a crescent moon had risen to light their way.

Kirkland stood in the bow. He was watching for Lost Island. Kirkland really believed that they could free Joey and Vinnie.

Miles didn't share Kirkland's confidence. Neither did Len. They were both hoping that they would miss Lost Island in the half-light. If they overshot their mark, they might get into the shipping lanes before Kirkland could complain.

"See anything?" Cruiser called to Kirkland.

Kirkland shook his head. "Not yet."

The whole gang had come along, including the new boys. Augie brought Commando with him. The boat was riding low in the water because of the extra weight. Miles worried that the vessel could overturn if they hit rough waves.

"There it is!" Kirkland cried.

He pointed toward the dark shapes in the distance. They could see the mountain of Lost Island, and they could hear the dull roar of the surf against the beach.

Kirkland gestured to the south. "All the way up, Bookman. Where the beach ends at the rocks."

"Aye, aye, Captain."

Kirkland resembled a pirate. His face was covered with green mud. He wore the crossbow strung over his shoulder.

He looked back at Miles. "You remember the plan?"

Miles nodded. "By heart."

"Don't get smart," Kirkland replied. "Just say it like I told you."

Miles sighed. "After we drop you on the beach, you and the others go through the jungle to Meat Hook's camp. Hayden and I go around the island and sail into the lagoon. We fire the flare gun to draw out the mutants. When they chase us, we run. You and the others free Vinnie and Joey."

Kirkland nodded. "I'll go in with Cruiser. Augie and D.J. will hang back in the trees in case something—just in case."

Augie frowned. "I want to go in with you!"

Kirkland pointed a finger at him. "You do what I say, kid."

Commando lifted his head to growl at Kirkland.

"No, boy," Augie told him.

Commando obeyed Augie, lowering his head.

"Wild," Len muttered.

Kirkland looked back at Miles. "Say the rest of it, Bookman. What happens after we free Vinnie and Joey?"

"We sail back to the beach and pick you up," Miles replied.

Kirkland nodded. "Okay, you got it. Now, put the boat on the beach."

Miles steered the vessel into the shorebreak. The hull rocked as the boat caught the wave. They were jolted when the bow hit the sand.

"Everybody out!" Kirkland cried. "Except the dweebs."

The four boys and the dog climbed out of the boat. They waded through the surf. Kirkland and Cruiser pushed the boat away from the shoreline.

"Give us an hour!" Kirkland shouted.

Miles nodded. The boat rocked in the waves for a moment. Then the sail billowed, and they rushed out into the night, leaving the others to disappear into the jungle.

"I hope they make it back alive," Miles said.

Len gazed back at his friend. "Let's split,

Bookman. Let's get out of here and leave those idiots."

"We can't."

"They don't care about us," Len said. "Besides, we can find help."

"No, Hayden. We've got to see it through. We can't leave them."

"They'd leave us."

"I know," Miles replied. "They would. But we wouldn't."

Len looked out at the dark water. "You're right, Bookman. You're always right."

The vessel swung around the southern end of the island. Miles steered the craft in a circular pattern. They had to wait for an hour without drifting away from the island.

"Have you got the flare gun?" Miles asked.

Len lifted the burlap bag with the supplies. "Right here."

"Dig a little deeper," Miles said.

"What?"

"Look in the bottom of the bag."

Len dug into the sack. He came up with a square leather pouch. It felt heavy in his hand.

"The lead weight," Len said. "You had me bring it from the compound."

"That's not lead," Miles replied. "It's an explosive charge. I found it in the secret chamber."

Len stared cautiously at the package. "Get out of here! You let me carry this without telling me what it was?"

121

"It's not armed," Miles told him. "I couldn't find a fuse. And I had to let you carry it. If Kirkland found out, he might've had a hemorrhage."

Len eased the charge back into the bag. "You mean we can't set it off?"

"Maybe with the flare gun."

Len whistled. "Good idea. If we need it."

Miles peered across the water at the dark island. "I have a feeling we will."

The ocean was calm and beautiful. A warm breeze kept the sail fully extended. The boys sat quietly as the minutes passed.

Finally Len looked back at Miles. "Has it been an hour yet?"

Miles peered at the crescent moon. "I think so."

Len clutched the flare gun tightly in his sweaty hand. "I still don't like this, Bookman."

"Neither do I."

They were silent for a moment.

"What do you think?" Len asked.

Miles nodded toward the dark shoreline. "Let's go in. We can't wait any longer."

Miles steered the boat toward the southeastern tip of the island. Moonlight spilled onto the water. They could see the high walls of rock that lined the outer bay. The rock hid the secret lagoon of the bandit camp.

Len was sweating. "I hope we can find that channel."

Miles felt his stomach turning. "Me, too."

They headed straight for the wall of rock, waiting for the hidden passage to open up and swallow them.

Kirkland lay low on his belly. His darkened face blended into the undergrowth. He could see the fire of the mutant camp.

So far, they had been able to get close to the camp without any trouble. Augie and his dog were back in the bushes with D.J. Their position was about a quarter-mile behind Cruiser and Kirkland.

Cruiser turned his head toward the older boy. "Where's Miles?"

Kirkland punched him. "Shh."

He could see the hanging cage where Joey and Vinnie were being held captive. They had to be quick—cut the rope and run.

"Come on, you guys," he muttered under his breath.

He had learned to trust Len and Miles. They had been through a lot together. The two preps had always been on time.

All Kirkland could do now was wait.

"Aw, crud!" Len cried. "We're stuck."

Miles looked forward. "Chill out," he whispered. "And keep it down. Your voice echoes."

The bottom of the sailboat scraped against a submerged rock. Miles pushed against the wall of rock that rose up beside them. "It's okay.

We've got to pull the boat along the wall. The tide is moving against us."

Using their hands, they got the boat moving again.

Len held his breath as they emerged into the lagoon. "This place gives me the creeps."

Miles gazed toward the fires that burned in the bandit camp. "Take it easy. Let's just do it and go."

Len aimed the flare gun. "Rockets away."

"No!" Miles replied. "We have to get closer."

"Yeah, yeah. I still say this is stupid."

"No arguments from me, Hayden."

Miles grabbed the tiller again. The sail filled with air. They started moving toward the beach.

"I'm going to swing toward their boats," Miles whispered. "Shoot when I give you the signal."

"I hope they haven't seen us."

"The camp looks quiet," Miles replied.

Len's heart was pumping. They never should have come. Kirkland's plan was going to get them all killed.

They saw the masts of Meat Hook's armada. The boats were resting on the beach. Len aimed the flare gun.

"Ready, Bookman."

Sweat dripped into Miles's eyes. "Wait!"

"We're almost on the beach!"

Another minute passed as they quietly drifted closer to the bandit camp.

"Now!" Miles commanded.

Len pulled the trigger. The flare streaked across the water. A sail caught fire on a catamaran.

A bandit sentinel raised a crossbow in their direction.

Len fumbled to reload the flare gun.

An aluminum arrow sailed over their heads. Len snapped the cartridge into place. He turned and fired a flare into the bandit's chest. The bandit fell to the ground, screaming.

A dull cry rose from the heart of Meat Hook's encampment.

"Well," Miles said, "they know we're here."

The bandit's scream still sounded in Len's ears. He was trembling. He didn't know how much more of this he could take.

When the first flare exploded, Kirkland jumped to his feet. "Let's go, Cruiser!"

The younger boy was frozen. Kirkland had to kick him. Cruiser rose on wobbly legs.

"I don't want to go in there, Kirkland."

"Shut up and move!"

They ran from the jungle onto the sand.

Kirkland saw the hanging cage. Joey and Vinnie were staring toward the burning boats. Kirkland knew he had to be quick.

The bandits were running around in the shadows. Kirkland held the crossbow in front of him and started for the cage.

Cruiser stumbled and fell. When Kirkland

reached back to pick him up, he realized then that Meat Hook's men were not as confused as they seemed.

Cannibal pointed toward Kirkland. "The children!"

Vinnie turned to look at his friends. "Kirkland! Cut the rope!"

A hail of arrows dropped suddenly around Kirkland and Cruiser. The bandits had seen them. They were reloading for another barrage.

"We can't make it!" Cruiser shouted.

Kirkland wanted to keep going, but a line of men emerged from the shadows. They were ready with their crossbows. Kirkland knew he couldn't take another step without dying.

"Run!" he cried. "Run for your life."

They turned back toward the jungle with bandit arrows flying past their heads.

The escaping sailboat drew closer to the channel between the rocks.

"The tide is moving again," Miles said. "We're going to make it away from here."

Len looked back. "Maybe not. Look."

Meat Hook's men were launching their boats to pursue them. They had catamarans. Their boats would be faster.

"We'll never be able to hold them off," Len said.

Their sailboat drifted into the mouth of the channel.

126

"Get the charge," Miles commanded.

Len was shaking. "What?"

"The explosive! It's in your sack!"

They let the tidal flow take the boat through the channel. Behind them, the bandits were crying out for blood. Several aluminum arrows fell just short of their stern.

When they reached the other end of the channel, Miles grabbed the rock wall. He steadied the boat, looking for a place to hang the charge. At last he found a pointed crag.

"Hand me the pouch, Hayden."

The bandits' voices echoed in the channel. They were getting closer. Miles hung the charge on the rocks and pushed the boat away. They headed into the outer bay, picking up speed.

"Use the flare gun, Hayden!"

Len aimed, but the pouch was too far away for him to see it. Still he had to shoot. The flare streaked across the bay. It hit the rocks above the pouch.

Miles grabbed the weapon from Len. He started to reload. They had to set off the charge, or the mutant fleet would surely catch them.

"They're getting closer, Bookman!"

The searchlights from the fleet reflected on the walls above the channel. The mutants were not going to give up easily.

Miles lifted the flare gun. "I hope this works."

The first flare was still burning above the

charge, so Miles could see the pouch. He took careful aim and pulled the trigger.

The flare streaked again. It was a direct hit this time. The intense light burned on the leather pouch.

"They're almost out!" Len cried.

The first bandit craft appeared at the mouth of the channel.

"No!" Miles cried. "One of them is reaching for the charge! If they put it out—"

"We're dead!" Len rejoined.

Just before the bandit could grab the pouch, the flare burned through to the explosives inside. A shock wave rumbled through the night air. Len and Miles were knocked down by the force of the blast.

Pieces of rock rained down around them. Smoke filled the air. When Len and Miles were finally able to sit up, they saw that the entrance to the hidden lagoon was no longer there. Rocky debris blocked the channel.

"They'll never get out of there!" Len yelled.

Miles grabbed the tiller. "No, but we will."

Len turned back to look at him. "Let's get away from here while we still can, Bookman."

"No," Miles replied. "We have to stick to the plan. Like it or not, we have to pick up the others."

"If they're still alive," Len said in a low voice.

The thorny jungle lashed at Kirkland's face. Cruiser ran beside him through the undergrowth. Fear strengthened their legs and catapulted them toward the beach.

Cruiser stumbled in the brush. Kirkland bent to pick him up. Their eyes stared back at the torches that burned in the hands of Meat Hook's men.

"They're monsters!" Cruiser screamed.

Kirkland stared ahead for a moment. "Augie! D.J.!"

There was no reply from the dark jungle.

"Keep moving," Kirkland told Cruiser.

A strident voice came from the torchlight. "They're over there!"

Kirkland lifted the crossbow. He pulled the trigger, sending a shaft through the darkness. The arrow lodged in the chest of a bandit. He fell to the ground, screeching in pain.

"You got one!" Cruiser said.

Meat Hook's own voice rose in the jungle. "Get them! Kill the foolish children! Cut their heads off."

Cruiser shook violently. "Kirkland!"

Kirkland urged him forward. The older boy didn't want to get caught. He would rather die than be locked in the bamboo cage.

"What about Augie and D.J.?" Cruiser said as they ran.

Kirkland couldn't think about the younger boys any longer. All he wanted to do now was save his own neck.

Arrows whizzed over their heads. They stumbled through the jungle without looking back. The bandits seemed to be gaining on them.

Miles held the tiller steady as the boat neared the beach. "You see them, Hayden?"

Len shook his head. "Not yet."

They had to make a decision quickly. The tide carried the boat toward shore. They were almost in the white froth of the shorebreak.

"Come on, Kirkland," Miles muttered to himself.

Len peered back at his friend. "Miles, they aren't coming. I know it. They aren't—"

"We've got to wait!"

"They'd leave us," Len replied. "They wouldn't wait for us."

Miles pointed toward the beach. "There!"

Kirkland and Cruiser broke from the jungle. They streaked through the moonlight. Len cried out and waved to them.

Miles turned the boat into the waves. The surf lifted the hull and the sailboat surged toward the sand.

Cruiser tripped again. Kirkland heard the snapping bone. Cruiser cried out, holding his ankle.

Kirkland bent to help him, but Cruiser couldn't get up. Kirkland would have to carry him.

The boat bumped against the shoreline.

"Hurry!" Len cried. "You better—no! One of them is hurt!"

Miles stared at the jungle. "They have company, too."

One of the bandits ran onto the beach. He started after Kirkland and Cruiser.

Kirkland turned to face the bandit and tried to reload the crossbow, but the string snapped.

The mutant aimed his own crossbow. "Time to die, children."

Suddenly he gave a loud cry. Something had leaped onto his back. Commando had charged from the jungle.

The dog's teeth dug into the bandit's neck. Blood poured over Commando's snout. The bandit fell to the ground, screaming.

Kirkland picked up the bandit's crossbow and sent an arrow through the fallen man's skull.

"Commando! Here!"

Augie ran up beside the dog. D.J. was right behind them. They could hear more of Meat Hook's men in the jungle.

Kirkland pointed toward the water. "Everyone in the boat."

The younger boys ran for the waves. Kirkland picked up Cruiser and carried him toward the boat. The younger boys climbed into the boat, followed by Commando. Len watched as Kirkland drew closer.

"I think Cruiser broke his ankle," Kirkland said.

Len helped Cruiser into the boat. "Is everyone here?"

"We couldn't rescue Vinnie and Joey," Kirkland replied. "The mutants got on us before we could free them."

Miles held the tiller in hand. "Hurry. Hayden, help Kirkland push us off."

Len jumped into the water. He and Kirkland pushed the vessel beyond the waves. Miles lifted the sail as they climbed over the side.

Kirkland peered out at the dark water. "Where's the fleet?"

"We blew up the channel," Len replied. "It's clogged with rock. They won't get out of there tonight."

Kirkland frowned. "Blew it up. With what?"

"I'll tell you later," Miles replied. "Right now we have to get out of here."

"We've got swimmers!" Kirkland cried.

Len looked back. He could see bandit heads bobbing in the lights. Kirkland reloaded the crossbow.

"I'll show them."

The bow twanged again. An arrow caught the first bandit's head. Kirkland missed the second time. The bandit drew closer as he fumbled with the crossbow.

"He's on us!" Len cried.

The bandit's hand gripped the side of the boat. Len cocked the flare gun. He fired the charge straight into the bandit's face.

"Good shot!" Kirkland cried. "He won't bother us anymore!"

The other swimmers got discouraged and turned back.

The boat knifed through the water. A stiff breeze had risen to propel them through the moonlit night. Miles started to turn the vessel east.

"No!" Kirkland cried, pointing north. "Back to the island. We have to take care of Cruiser's foot."

Miles grimaced. "Kirkland—"

"I mean it! Go back to the island, or you'll be sorry."

Miles shook his head in disgust. "How many times do I have to save your life before you trust me, Kirkland?"

"Just do it!"

Miles swung the tiller, obeying the brutish Kirkland.

Len sighed. The raid had been a bust. Vinnie and Joey were still captives. Kirkland was in charge again. Len thought they should have taken the boat when they had the chance. At least they could have saved their own hides.

"Holding steady," Miles said.

They sailed for a long time before they saw the shape of Apocalypse Island on the horizon. The mountains were visible in the moonlight. The peaks rose toward the stars like an old friend welcoming the boys back to their unwanted home.

Fifteen

The night breeze blew warm over the Honolulu airport. Lieutenant Branch Colgan waited by the arrival gate. He was in civilian clothes. Since he had two weeks' leave, he had not worn his uniform.

The jet taxied toward the terminal. When it stopped, the passengers began to deplane. Colgan watched them carefully as they filed by.

Colgan had never seen the man he was meeting, but he knew the man's reputation and he had talked to him on the phone. Colgan knew he would be in even deeper trouble than he already was if Commander Nickles discovered his scheme.

A lanky, aristocratic, dark-haired man strode toward the gate. Colgan straightened his posture. He was nervous.

The man's dark eyes fell on him. "Colgan?"

"Yes. Sir Charles Bookman?"

The man extended his hand. "Call me Charlie. Everyone does."

"Yes, sir. I mean, Charlie."

"That's better."

"You have luggage?" Colgan asked.

"Just my carry-on."

Colgan felt the awkward silence. "How did you find out about me?" he asked.

"I'm a journalist," Sir Charles replied. "And I have connections. It's my business to be nosy, especially in matters concerning my family. Suppose we go somewhere and have a cup of tea. Then you can tell me how you plan to help me find my son."

Vinnie gripped the bamboo bars as the cage rose over the dark camp. The mutants had taken Joey out of the cell. They were going to torture him again.

"You jerks!" Vinnie cried. "Leave him alone. You've hurt him enough!"

The bandits had formed a circle around Joey. They wanted blood. Kirkland's raid had left them eager for revenge. Vinnie figured the others had gotten away. The mutants hadn't brought any of them back to camp as prisoners.

Meat Hook leered at Vinnie. Bullet Head also stared up from the pack. When the circle parted, Vinnie saw Cannibal holding the bloody ax.

"No!" Vinnie cried. "You vultures!"

The bandits laughed at him.

Vinnie stared wide-eyed at the horror. Tears streaked from his eyes. He finally had to turn away from the spectacle.

Meat Hook raised Joey's head on a stake. "See what you foolish boys have wrought!"

Miles stood on the beach, staring toward the compound above. The sun was rising in the east. They had been waiting on the beach all night.

Len was lying in the sand. Kirkland knelt beside Cruiser, looking at his ankle. Augie, Commando, and D.J. were sleeping in a huddled heap.

Kirkland stood up. "We've got to get Cruiser to the lab. His ankle is swollen pretty bad."

Miles nodded. "Be careful with him. You don't want to make it any worse when you carry him."

Kirkland looked sideways at Miles. "Bookman—"

Miles turned away. "Forget it, Kirkland. Whatever you've got to say, I don't want to hear it."

Kirkland bristled. "What's your problem?"

"You're the only problem I've got," Miles replied. "We could have sailed east last night. Only you wanted to come back here to this hateful island."

"Just to fix Cruiser's ankle," Kirkland said. "That's it!"

"Right. You just wanted to be in charge."

136

"No," Kirkland said. "I mean it, Bookman. As soon as we fix him up, I'm all for getting out of here. We can blow off this horror show for good."

Miles's eyes narrowed. "You mean it?"

"Sure. As soon as we get ready, we can sail east. Just like you said."

"Why didn't you want to do it last night?" Miles asked skeptically.

Kirkland shrugged. "Well, we couldn't sail without food and water. Who knows how long we'll be out there before someone spots us?"

Miles figured that Kirkland was making some sense. "No weird stuff?" he asked.

Kirkland held out his hand. "I mean it. As soon as we can pack, we're out of here."

Miles clasped hands with him. "All right, Kirkland. But you better mean it this time."

"I mean it."

Miles looked at Cruiser. "We better get him up to the lab."

Len stood up. "I'll help," he said eagerly.

Len wanted to be off the island as badly as Miles. He wanted to hurry before Kirkland changed his mind.

Cruiser moaned, rolling his head. "It hurts."

"Not for long," Miles assured him. "We'll take care of you."

Kirkland bent down. "Okay, Hayden. You take his shoulders. I'll get the other end."

Miles turned to look toward the compound. "I think I saw some plaster in the Proteus room.

We can make a cast. I broke my arm once, and I think I can remember—"

No one had seen the arrow coming. The aluminum shaft thudded into Miles's side.

"I'm hit!" Miles cried.

He fell into the sand, blood pouring from the wound.

Kirkland stared toward the jungle. "There he is!"

Dog Face was running into the forest, the crossbow dangling from his hand.

Kirkland broke into a run, chasing Dog Face.

Miles tried to raise his head. He was gasping for air. The arrow protruded from his torso.

Len knelt next to him. "Hang in there, Bookman. You'll be all right."

Miles closed his eyes. His face had turned white. He shivered, and then his body went limp.

"No!" Len cried. "Don't die, Miles! Don't die!"

Will Miles live or die? Follow the boys' continuing adventures, when they are visited by a mysterious stranger, in Escape from Lost Island #3, **Mutiny!**